Papua: 1942–43

Papua: 1942–43

a novel

Charles Parker

iUniverse, Inc.
Bloomington

Papua: 1942–43

Certain characters in this work are historical figures, and certain events portrayed did take place. However, this is a work of fiction. All of the other characters, names, and events as well as all places, incidents, organizations, and dialogue in this novel are either the products of the author's imagination or are used fictitiously.

iUniverse books may be ordered through booksellers or by contacting:

iUniverse
1663 Liberty Drive
Bloomington, IN 47403
www.iuniverse.com
1-800-Authors (1-800-288-4677)

Because of the dynamic nature of the Internet, any web addresses or links contained in this book may have changed since publication and may no longer be valid. The views expressed in this work are solely those of the author and do not necessarily reflect the views of the publisher, and the publisher hereby disclaims any responsibility for them.

Any people depicted in stock imagery provided by Thinkstock are models, and such images are being used for illustrative purposes only.

Certain stock imagery © Thinkstock.

ISBN: 978-1-4620-1799-7 (sc)
ISBN: 978-1-4620-1801-7 (dj)
ISBN: 978-1-4620-1956-4 (ebk)

Printed in the United States of America

iUniverse rev. date: 5/10/2011

I dedicate *Papua: 1942-43* to those heroic Allied Forces who fought the battles of WWII, in and around Papua New Guinea, the Solomon Islands and the Philippines.
They made it safe for men, such as I, who came later.

PREFACE

Papua New Guinea is just north of Australia. Papua, and the Solomon Islands that are east of Papua, were the scene of some of the worst battles of World War II in the South Pacific. The interior of Papua is, even today, largely unexplored. A tall rib of mountains, the Owen Stanley Range, runs the length of Papua, isolating the two sides. Most of the developed area is on the shoreline, whereas the interior is characterized by formidable jungle, sparsely populated by indigenous tribes thought by some to still practice head- hunting.

As our story opens, the Japanese forces occupy much of the eastern shoreline and have destroyed a vital radio station needed by the Allied Forces for navigation. A daring mission to create a new station has left three people separated. This is their story.

CHAPTER ONE
JOE'S RECORD

This much I know: I fell out of the sky in a parachute. I was unconscious and I awoke from the boom of thunder followed by a refreshing downpour of rain. I was not on the ground. In fact, I was a very long way from the ground, perhaps a hundred feet up. My chute was hung up in an immense tree. The view down was sickening, and the view up was impossible because of the way I was dangling supported at my back. I knew I was in a parachute from the harness I was wearing, and I was sure that if the chute were to now break loose, it would be the end of me. I tried not to move more than to check myself for broken bones; there were none. My head, however, throbbed unmercifully!

By now the rain had stopped. I was in a stand of tall trees on a steep hillside, a jungle actually, and I soon became aware of monkeys chattering above me. I could see and hear a river roaring in the ravine off to my right. Where was I? Why was I here? As I pondered these questions it began to dawn on me that I no longer knew myself. This was almost more frightening than the fear of falling to my death. I looked at my hands. There was a gold band on my left ring finger – so I must be married. How could I forget my wife? Do I have children? There was a watch on my wrist, smashed beyond recognition. My name, surely that would come to me. This had to be a momentary lapse. So I thought, at the time, but I was wrong. After these eleven days it still escapes me.

I searched my pockets, which was not easy with the harness binding me. I found a handkerchief and checked my head for bleeding; there was a little. I found a candy bar and quickly devoured half of it; what bliss. I found a fountain pen, the one I am using now. My wallet, however, was missing; I must have had one. Had someone robbed me? Perhaps! These were the bewildering thoughts that swirled through my pounding head, until I mercifully fell into sleep, or perhaps I went into a coma.

Whatever it was, I awoke from it to the sound of human voices, and there far below me stood a group of men staring up at me. Hanging there asleep, I realized they must have thought I was dead. They were small of stature, dark skinned and wore little clothing. Each carried a long bow and had a quiver of arrows slung across his back, and yet they did not appear to be dangerous. I called down to them, "Can you help me?" and they responded enthusiastically in a language I could not comprehend. It was clear that they were pleased to find me alive and they appeared to be discussing how they might save me, but it was hard for me to imagine how they would do it. They walked about the surrounding trees looking up and doing a lot of pointing, until finally they sent a boy off on an errand while the rest squatted down to wait.

We tried talking to each other, all of us jabbering away, pretending to understand each other. We laughed and made signs and on a primitive level I know we were communicating friendship. Deeper understanding would come later. Finally we stopped chattering and just smiled at each other, and waited, and waited, and waited.

Waiting, however, was really getting difficult for me. I had to go! And I couldn't wait! I decided that since we were all men there, and before any women might possibly show up, I had to take action. I opened my fly and shouted a warning to the men below to move away from the target range. To my surprise, they all jumped up and cheered me as I relieved my bladder. These men felt my pain and felt my relief. Friends in need are friends indeed! It was then that I became certain that my life was in good hands and I would be rescued.

With little left to do physically, I settled down to serious efforts to regain my memory. I repeated every male first name I could think of, but none seemed to fit me. It seemed amazing that I could recall a list of names, but not my own. Giving up on that line of thinking for the moment, I tried the airplane I must have been in, or was it a balloon? Again: nothing. How could my brain selectively forget something so primary? I began to feel a kind of numbness pervade my entire being.

I am sure it was five or six hours before there was a shout through the forest, and suddenly the boy returned, bringing another man who carried a large coil of rope over his shoulder. This man was considerably taller and had the muscular appearance of an athlete. To my surprise, the first thing he did was to lie down full-length on his back and begin to stare up at me and at the surrounding trees. It is clear to me now that he was both resting and planning how to rescue me, but at the moment I felt as if I was being abandoned, and felt prompted to shout, "Please help me!" His response was to raise one finger in my direction and give me a big smile. This man was calling the shots.

Finally he stretched and sat up, which appeared to be the signal for the others to gather about him. There was much pointing and talking as my savior explained his plan to the others. There was a tree about fifty feet from the tree I was in that had more branches on the trunk than other trees which were closer by. The coil of rope was placed carefully at the base of this tree, each loop of the coil offset so that it would not snarl as it was extended. Now, walking to the tree and picking up the end of the rope, my savior made a small knot on the end and tossed it over the crotch of the first branch above him, a distance of maybe fifteen feet. Now, with his fist holding two thicknesses of rope, he hoisted himself up, hand-over-hand, inverted his body and slung his leg over the branch and with remarkable ease was soon sitting in the crotch. Again, he looked up at me, and with a grin simply raised one finger. This was a man of few words. I grinned back.

After a brief rest my hero repeated the procedure to reach the next crotch, and the next, and the next, until he was so far above me that I could no longer follow his progress. Now I realized that my friends on the ground were trying to tell me something, but before I understood, a loop of rope was crashing down on my head. I reached for it, but it slipped from my grasp and swung back to the other tree. On the second try, I caught it and found it to be made of carefully woven vines and the end was tied in a bowline knot making a loop for me to sit in. This man thought of everything.

As soon as I got the loop around my butt, my friend began to pull me up so that my weight gradually transferred to the rope and away from the parachute and I gradually approached the tree. I had not gone far, however, when suddenly the chute came loose and I was flying pell-mell toward that tree. Fortunately, I was traveling feet-first so that when I crashed into the trunk, I was able to spin myself off to one side and finally come to rest with my parachute dangling below me. The rest was simple: My friend would lower me to a crotch; he would reposition himself, and then lower me again until we reached the ground. Solid ground! Oh how good that felt. And, oh my, what a warm welcome I was given by my new friends.

Now that I was firmly on the ground, an old man took charge of my care. He ordered the others to stand back while he inspected me all over. I gathered that he was a medicine man and he gave me the full treatment. He checked me for broken bones, rubbed a green colored salve on my scrapes, and provided me water to drink from his leather flask. Finally, finding me fit to travel, he let the others approach me. Next I was fed a concoction that tasted like fermented spinach. It was horrible! I smiled and implied that I had only recently dined. I'm sure they saw right through me, but they took my rejection graciously. I was dying to eat the other half of my candy bar, but I felt very self- conscious about letting them see me doing it. I guess my mother must have trained me to be polite. I decided to wait until I could sneak a bite without being seen.

With all the formalities and expressions of friendship out of the way, it was time to head "home," wherever that was. My tree-climbing hero led the way, swinging a machete. I followed behind, the boy carried the parachute on his head behind me, and the rest followed after, single file. There were eight of us. I had no idea how far we had to walk. I was bone-tired, hungry, and ready to pack it in, but my new friends acted as if the day had only just begun. Actually night was fast approaching and I was beginning to have some desperate thoughts about getting them to stop, when suddenly we entered a small clearing that was apparently their campsite. I realized that these people knew their way around without any advice from me. They had saved my life so I had an obligation to be a patient guest.

The site had a low shelter about twenty feet long by ten feet deep with a thick thatched roof sloping to the rear. There were no sidewalls. Under the shelter each man had his space, with a woven mat for each to sleep upon. It was very neat and orderly, much like an army barracks. My parachute was placed at the end, after much shifting of the mats to make room, and much arguing among the men. I tried to indicate that I might sleep out in the open, but they would not hear of it. I was now one of them.

When it was all settled, the boy came to me and with a big grin, pointed to himself and said, "Kan." It was time to get acquainted and I had to provide some kind of name for myself. I simply could not admit I had forgotten my own name, so I gave it my best and blurted out, "Joe," even though I was sure that was not it. So Joe I became, and all the others in turn came to me and spoke a name. The handsomely built athlete who saved my life was something like "Guguloguda," but of the others, as I write this record several days later, I can only remember my young friend and helper, Kan. Kan has become my constant companion and soon I had a vocabulary of words which he taught me. In fact, even as I write this record of events, Kan is looking over my shoulder, embarrassingly close, fascinated by what I am doing.

Kan was about twelve or so, and he was clearly planning to be my companion and instructor. He was a handsome boy with an infectious smile and boundless energy. He would come running up to me, and standing very close, speak a word he wanted me to learn and with much pointing, show me what it means. It is working. I am learning enough words to get by. This has impressed the older men into thinking I am intelligent, whereupon they flood me with conversation that goes way over my head, proving to their satisfaction that I am not very smart after all. With Kan I have no such trouble.

But I have digressed from my account. The camp, which turned out to be one of a number of hunting camps used by these people, was soon alive with activity. Everyone seemed to have a specific job to perform. Before long there was a fire blazing in a fire pit (a safe distance from the thatched roof), water had been hauled, perhaps from the river, and a small wild boar was roasting, skin and all, on a spit over the fire. The acrid smell of burning hair was gradually giving way to the aroma of roasting pork. I sat upon my folded parachute watching the activities, head propped on my knees, trying desperately to stay awake. I had a strange sense of having been reborn, a full grown man-child, into a community of people who would be my "family" from now on, my previous life having disappeared, maybe forever. I had a lot to learn, but Kan was there to teach me.

It was dark now and the smell of the roasting boar was almost more than I could bear. Finally Guguloguda, whom I shall refer to as "G" from now on, went to the fire pit and without removing the boar, sliced off the blackened hide and cut off chunks of meat. Kan then pierced each with a pointed stick, and carried them to the men. It was like a weenie roast. I expected to be served first, as a guest of honor, but I was not. I came last along with Kan, who sat down beside me. I felt pleased that I should be treated as one of the family and that Kan was at my side.

This time I had no desire for that other half of my candy bar. The pork was delicious, well cooked, and almost more than I could eat. Kan gave me water to drink from his water bag, the skin of some animal, so, feeling quite content, I stretched out on my parachute and fell into a deep sleep. That is all I recall of that night, so I must have slept well.

When I awoke the next morning the sun was high enough for it to be late morning. I found Kan sitting upright beside me, waiting for me. Seeing I was awake he gave a shout and soon the others appeared. It was pretty clear that they had changed their plans in order to let me sleep. Such considerate men! "G" came to check me out, lightly touched the bump on my head that still throbbed. I tried to indicate that I was fine and raring to go. Smiling now, "G" gave me his raised finger salute and shouted something to the others.

Things moved quickly after that. I was fed another chunk of pork, cold this time. It appeared that the others had already eaten every last bit of the boar, saving this nice portion for me. Now they were anxious to hit the trail, so when the last bite entered my mouth, they all rose to their feet and shouldered their gear. One of them carried a strange looking animal, already gutted, and dangling on a string: this morning's catch, this evening's supper. This time Kan and I took our place at the rear of the column, a sign, I reasoned, that I was considered able to keep pace.

The trail we walked now was smooth and well worn. Every so often I got a glimpse of the river in the ravine to our left. Mile after mile it was still there. At one point the path led right down to the shore where I was delighted to find another camp similar to the one where we had spent the night. By now I was getting the picture: they had these campsites all over so there was always a place for them to spend the night.

The sun indicated that it was mid-afternoon. I was delighted to see everyone settle down for a rest and a drink of fresh water. The water in the river was fast moving and looked sparkling clean, so I drank deeply. My legs were very tired by now, but my head felt much better. It was snack time and out came the green fermented spinach. The others all seemed to love it, but I demurred, pulling out my crumpled half candy bar and eating it in front of them. They acted as if they felt sorry for me. This time I spread my parachute a little wider so Kan could lie on it too. That pleased him and soon we were both spread out, side-by-side, on our backs.

"G" took only a short rest, flat on his back, before leaping to his feet and shouting for us all to do the same. Not wanting to be a pariah, I staggered to my feet too, only to find the medicine man by my side, checking me out to see if I was fit to travel. He felt my legs and peered into my eyes. He gently touched my head and then shook his head – travel was off for rest of the day. "G" acted put off by this news, but acquiesced. "G" was clearly not the man in charge.

Well, "G" was the only unhappy one. In no time at all, several men were standing in the river using their bows and arrows to spear fish (with incredible success), Kan was swimming and skipping stones, and someone else was getting a fire started. I waded in the shallow water for a while then decided to do it right – tore off all my clothes and joined Kan in the deeper water. It was glorious to feel cool and clean again. I was so pale compared to Kan and the others as I dried off with the sun feeling nice for a change. Poor "G," he just sat alone on a boulder and sulked.

That evening we dined well on fish and that strange animal they had caught that morning. That night we had a bright moon and the musical sound of the river to put us to sleep. It seemed so peaceful here, but there were dangers about that Kan described to me with hand gestures. Each night two of the men took turns doing guard duty, and keeping a fire going to frighten off night-hunting animals. In addition, all of the men kept their bows by their side at the ready in case the alarm was given. For me, very tired from walking, I slept really well.

The next morning, at dawn, Kan shook me awake. I was no longer a guest and they would not waste time letting me sleep. Waking up was made much easier by the aroma of more fresh fish cooking over the fire. Getting up from my parachute-bed, I staggered over and joined the group by the fire. It felt good in the early morning chill. The medicine man came over and felt me all over and seemed to give me a clean bill of health. In return, I gave him a big smile. As if this were a signal, all of the men began talking to me and laughing and I was doing my best to respond, when Kan settled beside me and responded for me. I heard the name "Joe" several times and the laughing stopped. I don't know what Kan said, but I suspect he was saying that I was some very important person and deserved more respect, because now they were all bowing in my direction. It was very embarrassing. Kan was putting me up on some pedestal from which I was bound to fall off.

Soon the fish was passed around. I was handed an extra large chunk on a big leaf, which I ate with my fingers as others did. It was dark and oily, like mackerel. It was very satisfying, but I had been given more than my share and this disturbed me. Perhaps it was due to the VIP status that Kan appeared to be promoting for me. I would need to straighten Kan out about that. I didn't have long to contemplate these matters, however, because as the last bite of fish entered my mouth, I looked up and found "G" glaring down at me and the whole group lined up ready to move on. I was holding up progress again! As soon as I scrambled to my feet, "G" shouted the order to move out. That ended my leisurely breakfast by the campfire.

This time the path veered away from the river, climbing quite steeply into a region of steep hills, mounds really, with the path passing in a zigzag manner between them. They reminded me of yet-to-be unearthed Mayan temples in the Yucatan Peninsula. What a thrilling thought! How had I known that? Had I been there? Was my memory returning? Was I in the Yucatan now? The possibility of my mind finally clearing so occupied my thoughts that I was stumbling along in a daze. Not paying proper attention to the path, I caught my toe on a rock and fell. Then to further my humiliation, the doctor made us all pause while he checked me over again with "G" fuming at the head of the line. I vowed to never let it happen again; it was time for me to shape up.

By noontime we had reached another campsite, this one beside a cold spring that bubbled out of the mountainside. The air was much cooler here, really quite comfortable and free of insects. All the men laid down their gear, rushed to the spring for a cool drink and partook of their vile "spinach delight" before lying down for a short nap. Kan, bless his heart, knew that I had eaten the last of my candy bar earlier so, after the others were settled, he motioned me aside. Kan carried a leather pouch at all times. Now, acting very secretive, he took from his pouch a strange fruit, pink in color, like a small grapefruit. Peeling one section off, he passed it to me and took another for himself. Following his lead, I bit into it and found it to be tart and sweet, a bit like lemonade, with a hard fiber-laden nut at the center. When I began to exclaim how good it was, he hushed me up. He didn't want to share his prize with the others. Seeing that I liked it he tore off another segment and passed it to me. No truer friend had any man! By the time that was consumed and the nut sucked dry, I felt quite satisfied.

As Kan and I sat on my parachute resting, I resisted the temptation to lie back and go to sleep so that I was ready when "G" gave the order to move on. I was learning. "G" was in a better mood now too, often shouting and singing in a strange tuneless manner. Perhaps an hour later, one of "G" 's shouts was answered from hills ahead of us and the entire group began to trot – we were almost home.

Soon the path ahead was filled with women and children, the greeting party, all happy to see their men return. The women wore thickly woven grass skirts that made them look short and fat. They were all bare-chested, some with a baby nursing away. The children, and there was quite a number, were all quite naked and soon were all crowded around me. I must have been a very strange sight. I kneeled down and held out my hand, but they just stared. I was pleased to see that they seemed unafraid, simply curious. As I began to take in the whole happy scene, I saw "G" with his arms about a young woman, maybe his wife. I could tell from his pointing and from hearing my new name, Joe, being spoken that he was describing my rescue. Now the women all came to be introduced. Kan stood proudly by my side and did all the talking, speaking each of their names, or so I assumed. All I had to do was smile and they smiled back.

I was not the star attraction for long, however. We began moving en masse now, the children running ahead, until we reached a clearing at the top of the hill. Several tall trees stood at the center of the cleared land with a large platform lashed between them, about fifteen feet above the ground.

Several tiny thatched roof huts were built on this platform forming a village in the sky. Access was by a flimsy looking ladder. Off to one side, on solid ground, stood a rather large open sided building with a thatched roof. It appeared that this was their center for cooking and gathering, while the village in the sky was for sleeping. Then, further over, stood four individual huts, built on stilts. These were larger; VIP quarters, perhaps. Beyond these I could see what appeared to be a large vegetable garden. Over the entire area, brown-feathered chickens roamed at will, clucking, and acting very much in charge.

Smoke curled up from one end of the large building and along with it a delicious aroma of roasting meat, and it was to this that the entire group was rushing. Here I expected to be taken and introduced to the women who were tending the roasting, but instead, Kan excitedly pushed me in the direction of "G" who was standing beside the ladder leading to the platform. He was impatiently waiting for me to follow him. He pointed with one finger – UP! Well, up he went, proving that the bamboo ladder was a lot stronger than it looked. Kan held me back until "G" had reached the top, then motioned me to follow. After I reached the platform, Kan practically flew up the ladder to join us. I kept back from the edge feeling a bit as if I was on a trampoline, since the entire platform moved erratically as we walked. The surface was constructed of bamboo strips with an underpinning of bamboo poles set close together in the opposite direction.

"G," still looking impatient, raised his finger again, this time pointing between the first two huts. It was tight, but we all slipped through by moving sideways. There were seven huts in all, all crowded on this swaying platform. They were round, about eight feet in diameter with tall conical thatched roofs. The walls were about four feet high of woven sticks with a mud adobe smeared on the surface to keep out the breezes.

Stopping at the entrance of the last hut, "G" pointed – IN with his finger, stooped low and entered the tiny doorway. I followed with Kan at my heels. It took a few seconds for my eyes to adjust to the dark interior and I found I could stand upright as I moved closer to the center. There, almost at my feet, lay a man dressed in what appeared to be a tattered army uniform, although no insignia was visible. He lay on his side, apparently asleep, with his face turned toward the wall. His breathing was raspy and erratic giving the impression that he might be ill. As I took this all in, my mind began to race with ideas. I leaned forward to get a better look at the man's face. He appeared to be Asian, possibly Japanese, and a man from the "outside," a man I might be able to communicate with. As I stood back up and faced "G" and Kan, their faces seemed to express the same hope. Perhaps they had provided me with an interpreter.

Speaking in low tones, "G" said something to Kan who immediately left the hut. Then pointing to me and then to the floor, "G" mimed sleep, making it quite clear that this was to be my sleeping quarters. Soon Kan reappeared carrying my parachute and a mat of dried grass, confirming that Kan and I were to be rooming right there. After placing the bedding on the floor there was little room left to spare, but judging from Kan's expression, it was a great improvement over what he once had. Despite all our moving about, however, the man on the floor slept soundly on.

Pointing – OUT now, "G" led the way down to the ground to where the women were preparing food. Kan and I were at his heels, eager for supper. Since we were arriving later than the others much of the roasting meat had been cut away so the identity of the creature was hard to determine. The aroma was not boar; that I knew. As my mind considered the other possibilities I realized that it was best not to delve into such matters if I wanted to enjoy the feast. "G" led the way, using a machete to slice a chunk of meat from the slowly turning animal and spearing it with one of the pointed sticks that lay nearby. The heat from the glowing embers was so intense that when I reached over to remove a slice, I had to back away. Kan was there to help, however – so young and yet so tough. He calmly reached over that inferno, sliced me a huge chunk plus one for himself, all with practiced ease. Kan, my salvation and friend!

Well, it was a delicious meal and the festivities lasted well into the evening. I noticed that one of the women carried food up to the platform, apparently for our sick companion. Kan remained close by my side, bringing me more meat and a mild brew served in cups made from bamboo. Bamboo, what wonderful things you can make from it. Two men played music (I guess one could call it music) using a bamboo flute and a bamboo drum. All this caused "G" and others to sing (off key) and shout, and prance about. It was quite a party.

It had been a long day, so when Kan tapped me on the arm and mimed sleep, we left the gathering and climbed the ladder to our hut. Fortunately, there was a bright moon that night making the interior of the hut dimly lit as well. Our companion was still in the same position, still breathing heavily. A large leaf with a slice of meat, apparently untouched, lay beside him. I moved my parachute bed close to the far wall with Kan next to the door. Smoke drifting up from the cook fire and, perhaps, the elevation of the platform, freed the air of the insects that were so annoying down below. It was heavenly and I was soon asleep.

When I awoke I found that both Kan and our companion were missing. Early morning sun was streaming into our hut and I felt a sudden rush of energy. I was eager to greet the new day. In addition I needed a toilet, and very soon. I rose, bent low at the waist and exited the hut. There, resting against the wall of the hut sat Kan and our companion enjoying the morning sun. Kan, seeing my need, leapt to his feet and pointed out the communal toilet, a slit trench, some distance from the living area. Turning now to our companion I gave him a welcoming smile, only to be greeted by an expression of sheer terror. He was clearly afraid of me.

I found the slit trench, which, despite the total lack of privacy, seemed to be otherwise quite civilized, with plenty of soft earth to kick on top. Returning to the hut, I hoped to improve my image with our companion. I wondered if he had suffered some derangement from his illness. As I approached, I offered my hand saying, "Hello, my name is Joe. I hope you are feeling better today," hoping he might understand. He made no reply, but his expression implied some recognition of what I had said. Still the fear lingered and it seemed to be directed at me, not at Kan who stood beside me. The man was Asian, barely twenty years old, although I had initially mistaken him as older because of his straggly beard. He was very thin and frail, about five foot six, and he had jet-black hair that contrasted with his pale skin. He certainly did not look well.

His obvious fear was disturbing so I tried to change the subject, signaling to Kan that I was thirsty and maybe our companion needed a drink too. Kan was off like a shot and I sat down where Kan had been sitting, close to the man in case he chose to speak. I spoke the word "Food", and rubbed my stomach. He responded by shaking his head. Progress!

I decided not to push it. We were both guests here, both from the "outside" so we should get acquainted slowly. No need to rush it – but maybe there was. He did not look healthy. I looked away from him to the trees, such beautiful trees that would shade us when the sun got higher. Now the sun felt lovely, friendly, so I closed my eyes. Soon Kan returned with a basket slung over his shoulder. He had brought us water and pastry that resembled a cross between a pancake and a Danish, but with a flavor that disappointed me. Being hungry, I ate mine; my companion did not. Then, signaling that I could call him, Kan raced off again, leaving us alone once more.

By now the sun felt too hot, so I moved to a shady spot and to my great surprise my companion moved over beside me. He was making advances! Since he had appeared to understand a bit of the English I had spoken before, I gave him a condensed version of my rescue from the tree, speaking slowly and using simple words. My companion said nothing, but his facial expression showed keen interest. I was making progress. He pointed to the bump on my head and finally spoke his first words, softly, and in PERFECT ENGLISH, "I hope that will not become infected. Ask the medicine man to use his green salve. It contains aloe, I think, and is quite effective. Is it still painful?"

Seeing that I could barely contain my surprise and glee, he put a finger to his lips. He looked around as if someone might hear us. This was to be our secret – but why? What was this man afraid of? In a hoarse whisper I said, "You speak English! This is incredible! Who are you? Where are we?" I was so excited I was stammering.

"Calm down and I'll tell you," he said, keeping his voice just above a whisper. "I am a wanted man, a deserter, and if I were captured I would be tortured to death. It is better I die here, when my time comes, and be fed to the vultures that circle overhead."

Frankly, that shocked me. "A deserter? From what and where is this jungle?" I said. My voice was rising and I felt his restraining hand on my knee.

"Joe, if that is the name they call you now, you and I are presumably arch enemies. I say, 'presumably' because, if you are an American as I'm sure you are, our countries are locked in a deadly war, which you seem to know nothing about. You may kill me when I explain it to you, you probably have that right, but I do not think you will." He paused there and waited for this to sink in. It did not. I kept quiet.

"I am Japanese," he said and here he lowered his head as if in great shame.

"What of it? I figured you for Asian, so what's wrong with that?" I murmured.

Now, straightening his shoulders and looking me straight in the eye, he said, "I bear the shame of my country, my people, for what they did. It was they, my people, who bombed Pearl Harbor in a sneak attack, a terrible, terrible act for which I must share some blame. This – you never heard of this – how strange! Does the name Adolf Hitler mean anything to you? We, my people, joined an unholy alliance with this Hitler to enter World War Two against America and you have forgotten all this. How strange."

He was quiet for several minutes as if uncertain about saying more. Then after a long sigh, he continued. "My name is Kato Matsuri. Long before all this began I was a carefree student at Harvard. My parents had sent me to the United

States and I was in my junior year studying medicine when I made the fatal mistake of returning to Japan to visit my parents, just before the war broke. Once there I could not return and was conscripted into the Japanese army, even though I was actually a US citizen. I was very upset so when our detachment came here to New Guinea – this is Papua, the eastern half of New Guinea, near Lae harbor, I left my post on guard duty and ran for my life. Now you know where you are and why I am on the run. That was months ago and I have no idea how the war is going or if my parents are alive." Here he stopped and seemed to be overcome with tiredness. "I must lie down," he said, and immediately staggered into the hut to rest.

My first reaction to this great flood of information was to repeat it over and over in my mind. I must not forget what I'd heard. This I knew could lead to more memories. Was I a soldier, an American? I pondered that strange line where memory ended. I had a reasonable knowledge of the world and its geography and I knew that Papua was the eastern part of New Guinea, probably from schooling as a child – but who on earth was I, and what had brought me to this place? I could feel my head spinning. How could I remember one, but not the other? I should seek out the medicine man for more green salve on my head as Kato suggested. As my bruise healed so would my mind.

I was sitting there in the shade struggling with these thoughts, when I felt the platform begin to tremble – I had a visitor. It was just the man I wanted to see, the medicine man, the doctor "doing his morning rounds." Behind came Kan, a medicine man in training, carrying the pot of green salve. My head was soon a matter of great discussion between them, with much touching and gentle tapping, followed by a fresh application of salve, this time by Kan, the trainee. It felt cool and fresh and I expressed my appreciation so there were grins of pleasure all around.

Next came Kato and I followed them into the hut to observe. This time Kan kept back as the medicine man felt his pulse and temperature and did a lot of stomach rubbing. Finally he gave him medicinal leaves to chew. This time the mood was somber. They called him by a different name, something like "Sunday." (This was a man in hiding.) After the others left I knelt down by my new friend and whispered, "Kato," whereupon he opened his eyes, shook his head and smiling, whispered, "I'm 'Sunday' – got it? I see they treated your head. That's good. Now, Joe, I need to sleep." So I left him, knowing I now had a confidant and friend.

Day 11: Today as we sat and talked, eleven days after my rescue, I mentioned to Kato my fear of having more memory loss and my wish to keep a written record. Smiling, he said, "I have just the thing. My mother gave me a journal book as I left for war. I never wrote in it because I always planned an escape, but I kept it because Mother wrote a prayer on the flyleaf. Now it will be yours, my friend." Thus begins my record of events as they happen. (Due to lack of space, my actual journal notes were short, but were invaluable, much later, for recalling events and writing this fuller account.)

Day 12: Today it is raining very hard. It is a fine day for recalling what happened during the past eleven days and entering it in my new journal. Kan is beside me, totally absorbed in the process of writing. He was especially thrilled to see his own name and has copied it on his arm to show others. He is so eager to learn words that I have started him with a copy of the alphabet scratched on the hut wall. He has been standing there, pointing to a letter and sounding it out, then peeking over at me to see if he got it right. He is learning fast!

Kato is sleeping soundly, covered against the chill by the furry skin of an animal. Today he has eaten some of the food that Kan has brought us. That seems like a good sign.

Day 13: The rain has stopped and as I looked down this morning from the vantage point of our platform, I could see that the entire compound was very well drained. Along the far side the land dipped before rising to even higher elevation beyond. A small stream flowed here and along side of it I could see a pipe of bamboo sections that conducted water to a huge tub near the kitchen, which in turn overflowed back into the stream. I asked Kan about this and he explained that it went to a spring high on the mountain to ensure pure water for drinking. I was impressed!

Day 15: This morning I was invited to join a fishing party in the big river. I expected they meant the campsite where we had previously been, but Kan indicated that it was much closer and more exciting. As we started out I saw that my companions were the older boys of the tribe, Kan being the youngest. The medicine man was with us too and "G" let the way.

The jungle that we passed through now was extremely dense, and the narrow winding trail was often bridged over with low hanging vines. Kan, my constant guardian, advised me to watch for snakes in the branches. After about thirty minutes of this I began to hear the roar of the river, previously muffled by the vegetation, growing louder and louder as were got closer. Suddenly "G" gave a shout. We were stopped on a narrow ledge at the edge of a rocky precipice and the river was far below us. I could see large shelving boulders that reached far out into the surging water and caused the current to flow in a large "S" pattern. The scene was both beautiful and terrifying! I clearly had a fear of height. I was beginning to feel dizzy and to wish I had not come on this adventure, when I felt Kan's steady hand on my arm gently leading me to a large rock where I could sit. He made it quite clear with hand signals that I was to stay there while he descended the cliff. Soon the medicine man came too, gave me a knowing smile, and sat down beside me. We would watch the show from here, together, safely, and in comfort.

"G" and the others disappeared around a bend in the ledge and reappeared minutes later on the rocks below. There were six of them and they took positions spread out along the bends of the river. Now they worked as a team. "G," standing on a rock, upstream of the others, would shoot a passing fish with his bow and arrow. If he hit one he would shout to Kan who stood at the first bend and acted as a spotter. When the fish came by he pointed it out to one of three older boys, the catchers, who took turns diving in to retrieve it. The catcher, fish in-hand, would be swept by the raging current to the next bend. There, the last boy helped him ashore using a bamboo pole. He would remove the arrow and bag the fish while the catcher ran back for another catch.

What a show! It was delightful to see my old companion, usually so serious, laughing and slapping his knee as each fish came ashore. The sun was high in the sky when the fishermen climbed back to the ledge with a full catch and we all trouped back to camp. There, the women took charge and the menu that day was fish, all you could eat!

Day 20: It is easy to see how quickly we have settled into a routine, especially with Kan eagerly caring for our every need. Kato, or shall I call him "Sunday," seldom leaves the platform except to use the slit trench, whereas, I have joined the activities of the camp, such as gathering firewood and repairing thatch on roofs. I now have a tan to rival any of the rest. I am blending in; I am going native.

Whenever Kato and I can be totally alone he tells me about the places he has known, and about his country of birth, Japan. He also teaches me about the country that may be the country of my birth, the United States of America. Much of this I already know, as well as the history and geography of many other countries – of the world, in fact. I must have been a good student in school. But despite this I cannot recall myself, or my place in that world. All my personal history is missing. And how can I have forgotten a war! Perhaps I was also a soldier who is absent without leave, but Kato said that if I was a soldier my hair would have been shorter and I would have a uniform. It is all so tantalizing and frustrating.

Day 32: Kato was quite certain that he had identified his disease as one, rare in the civilized world, but common here. He said the name, but I cannot recall it now. The herbs and leaves he was being fed seemed to help him sleep, and sleep gradually made him better. The swelling on my head had nearly disappeared, as well as the discomfort. So physically we were both getting better. Kato had lost track of time during his illness so neither of us knew the true date, but he knew the year to be 1942, and that it was fall in this hemisphere. Were we going to spend the rest of our lives here? Well, despite the fine treatment of these lovely, simple people, we both wanted fervently to return to the life we knew. Kato had a fiancée in the States, a young Japanese-American named Virginia, and he missed her dearly. I wanted to return to the man I was and be reunited with the wife I had forgotten. Until the war was over, however, we were safer where we were.

As Kato gradually recovered his health, he became less fearful of detection and allowed Kan to join our discussions and share some of our secrets. This pleased me greatly because we needed Kan as our ally. He had a wealth of information on tribal matters. Kan explained to us the organization of the tribe. "G," he explained, was the headman and made all decisions for the tribe, except, that is, when the elders felt required to disagree with him. I had seen the medicine man, one of the elders, pull rank on the "great one" myself. Not a bad system of government, really.

Day 73: Kato and I were enjoying the morning sun, when the platform began to shake violently, and seconds later Kan burst upon us, trembling and out of breath. He had been on a hunt with "G" and others on one of the hunting trails, when they saw a line of men, all dressed alike and carrying guns. They tried to hide, but "G" was not quick enough and was hit by a bullet in his leg. Despite the pain, "G" had run back to the village to warn the women and children to hide in the jungle. We must hurry! "Men come! Men come!" Kan whispered.

I went down the ladder first, followed by Kato and Kan. "G" was in the long house, blood streaming from his leg, urging the women and children to flee in the jungle as fast as they could run. I ran to aide "G," but he shook his head and pointed to the cover of the jungle. When we had run perhaps a mile, "G" withered and collapsed to the ground, thoroughly spent. Kato, Kan and I dropped to our knees beside him. There was no sign of the medicine man, but Kan acting as interpreter explained that Kato was a doctor too. "G" gave Kato a questioning look, but lay back on the ground and pointed to the wound. It was a deep flesh wound and the bullet had to be removed to prevent infection. Fortunately the bone was not broken, and for his comfort, "G's" pretty little wife/girlfriend sat on the ground cradling his head.

First Kato made a simple tourniquet from his own shirt, to stem the bleeding. Then, locating a bamboo patch, and using "G's" machete made a tool that resembled a soda straw. With this he entered the hole made by the bullet. "G" grimaced in pain because the flesh had closed around the hole. It was now that Kato put me to work. I was to lightly press the straw against the bullet and suck with all my strength, gradually drawing the bullet out. If all I got was blood, I was to stop and try again. It took many tries and much massaging of his leg, but the bullet eventually popped free. I was so dizzy I nearly fainted, but finally I had done something to repay that big man for saving my life, and I am sure Kato had similar feelings. When I showed the bullet to "G" he studied it for some time, smiled, then slipped it into the pouch he always carried. Maybe it became a good luck charm.

Kato would loosen the tourniquet just enough to let some blood flow, then stem it, until the blood began to clot. Then, as if on cue, the venerable old medicine man arrived with his little pot of green salve and collapsed beside us. Kan immediately moved to his side and explained what Kato and I had done for "G" and the old man appeared greatly relieved. He watched as Kato treated the wound with the salve to prevent infection and nodded his head in approval.

It later became clear that the medicine man had risked his life to save "G." Having run only a short distance, he returned in order to retrieve his precious pot. By this time the compound was swarming with soldiers so he hid at the edge of the clearing. Then, just as quickly, they all left, running in fact, taking a trail to the south. According to gestures made by the medicine man, the soldiers appeared to be running in fear. It was a strange, but encouraging report.

With the pressure off of me, I was able to rest back and take in the whole scene. There were perhaps twenty-five of us, squatting or sitting close together in the dense undergrowth. Except for an occasional whimper from one of the babies, everyone remained very quiet and alert. These were people familiar with danger. I noted that the men all faced outwards on alert. The jungle sounds were muted; all was well. In low whispers I was told we would remain there tonight, but there would be no fire, no hot food. The girls would search for fruit or berries during the day. Scouts would return to the compound tomorrow at daybreak to check. It would be a long night!

Kato signaled it was time to talk. The bullet he had removed was a 30 caliber of Japanese manufacture, slightly different than the US design. This was a detachment of Japanese, apparently in retreat. Could the war have turned? Kato was trembling with excitement. I placed my hand on his shoulder. "Don't jump to rash conclusions," I said.

As expected, it was a hard night. The young men formed a ring around the group, facing out, on guard. The rest of us tried to get a little sleep. At daybreak, "G" told scouts to investigate the compound and report back. When we were told that it was safe to return, "G" began to stand, only to be ordered, in no uncertain terms, to lie back down by the medicine man. A gurney of bamboo and vines, apparently constructed during the night, was placed beside "G," which he meekly crawled onto. It was sad really, to see the great one feeling so humiliated. Thus it was that we all trooped back to the compound to renew life again.

CHAPTER TWO
MATTIE'S DIARY

2/22/42 What a day this has been! The radio is just full of that attack on Darwin. Over 200 dead! What will happen to us! I am glad we live in Melbourne. And today, on Sunday no less, I began my new job at ComCen. They, I guess I should say "we," took over the old pottery plant. The sign is still on the front of the factory, maybe to fool the enemy. The "enemy," what a frightening word to write. I've always liked the Japanese, at least those that we know. Rick has several in his classes. They must be devastated and how will the others treat them. Children can be so cruel sometimes. I must ask Rick about them. And the gardener at the flower market, always so helpful. What will happen to him?

This whole thing, this diary I'm writing I mean, is Rick's idea. He says that the day will come when we will be glad we kept a record. He is probably right. It is better than sitting here tearing my hair out. The funds for my study of fauna in Tasmania have been cut off due to this war, so I should count myself lucky to land the job at ComCen. Tomorrow is my first full day on the job. Today was orientation, bathroom location, breaks and what not to tell ANYONE. Keeping my mouth shut will be a pill, that's for sure.

Rick will be home soon and I haven't begun supper. Maybe I'll serve burgers, salad and a cold beer, under the grape arbor. Sounds good to me. Out there we can usually get a breeze. Heavens, it has been a hot summer, and so dry. I hear there are fires in the outback. At ComCen they have large fans in every room to offset the heat made by all the radio and phone systems. I plan to dress light.

So who are we, in case someone besides family reads this stuff? Rick and I were married last October in Sydney, October eighth, to be exact, just Mum and Dad and Aunt Bess standing by. Rick, being a Yank, had no one. Long trip from the States and his mother not well. Now I am Mrs. Richard Billings, or Matilda, (as in "Waltzing Matilda"), or Mattie Jones Billings. Take your pick. Mum is a true Aussie, but I wish she had used more imagination in naming me. Every time I hear "Waltzing Matilda" I turn blue! I am glad Rick loves me, despite my name. If you are to believe him, I'm real cute. Oh yes, I am also a botanist.

Rick, now, he is a real hunk. Six foot one and all muscle. He is currently a geography, history and political science teacher at Melbourne Academy, plus all the things he does at the airfield, maintaining engines and flying all over the map. Helps to be good at geography. He has taken me up and it's fun. He came to Australia working for a big US company, but he prefers I not mention the name. Then he met me and stayed. Tough luck for the US of A!

Sometimes I get a stiff neck from looking up at him, because I am so short and he is so tall, and SO good lucking. He reminds me of Gary Cooper, the actor, only better. It is his quiet calm manner and the polite way he talks that resembles

Cooper more than his face. He has mischievous eyes that always look as if he has a surprise for you. I just adore those eyes! And he never lies, that is another thing. And those arms, God what arms!

How did I find this wonderful guy? It was pretty wild, really. This is how it happened. I was still living with Mum and Dad in Sydney and Mum had knitted a huge box full of mittens, caps and sweaters for the aborigines. It was July eleventh last winter, and it was freezing rain outdoors! Well I just happened to walk into the hall and saw Mum by the front door preparing to carry that box to the post office. I shouted, "Wait Mum. Don't go out in this weather! Here, let me take it, if it has to go today."

"Yes," she said. "It has to go today and I can take it. Do you see how awful the weather is? Those people need warmer clothes and there is no time to waste!" Well we argued back and forth as usual, but stubborn as she is, I finally won. I bundled up and headed down the block and a half to the post office with the box under a waterproof cover. There were very few people out and about, but a tall man was walking in my direction and just as he got close, my feet went out from under me! The man reached out to catch me, but we both went down together. He got up first and helped me to my feet. My nose was bleeding and my knee was beginning to hurt, but finding myself in the arms of this man, I began to laugh which got him laughing too. He was beautiful. I told him I was fine, but he didn't think so. He picked up my box and insisted on turning around and walking with me to the post office. I was limping and he let me use his arm as support. When the postmistress saw us she brought out two chairs so we could sit near the heater and she gave me a bandage for my nose.

Again I suggested that I was OK and thanked him, but chemistry had begun to work and he stayed right where he was. We had already introduced ourselves, but now we got down to the nitty-gritty, getting to really know each other. The more I heard about Rick, the way he thought, the things he liked, the more I wanted to hear. I told him things I would never have told anyone else, not any other man surely! Every so often I would glance over to the postmistress and she would give me a very knowing smile – she knew what was going on.

Up to that day I had dated a lot of men, mostly in college, but I never met one that warranted more that a couple dates. They all seemed to be seeking "love," while I was looking for friendship and fun. I spent more energy trying to end relationships than start them. One girl friend said I was leaving a long trail of broken hearts. From my viewpoint, the men I had met all had the wrong expectations. But that was then; Rick seemed so different, so genuine, so considerate, so real! Was I falling in love?

When the postmistress finally came to us and said she had to close the office in half an hour, Rick went to get his car so he could take me home in comfort. When we got to our house I invited him in to meet Mum and Dad. Mum had been terribly worried and was teared-up a little, but smiling! Dad said, "So that's why you were gone so long. Glad to meet you, Rick. I was just about to have a beer, would you like one?" It was a good beginning.

That is how it all started. We dated a lot after that and every date left me wanting more. He is my man and I am so glad we got married. I love him to pieces! (Oops, time to leave the typewriter and do supper.)

2/23/42 Rick was very moody last night. Supper outside was a good idea until the bugs got too bad. We could use a screened porch. Tonight I told him about my first full day at work, but no secrets. Today I was a phone operator, learning the ropes of how to patch through calls and keep everyone happy, even when they scream obscenities in your ear! There are about twenty women doing that, all working like crazy, while the men are setting up more stations in another room. Apparently more women will be added soon. There are three eight-hour shifts around the clock. I got the day shift this month, evening next and so forth. Every eighth day we have a day off. I can say this: By lunch break I was so tired, and with only half an hour you choose between your sandwich and a nap; there's no time for both.

After I have done this work for a few months I may be put on radio communications. That comes with a pay increase so it must be even harder. I have added my name to a list so let's see what happens. Rick thinks I'm too daring, but says he is very proud of me. (Maybe I can get him to do supper sometimes.)

3/1/42 Finally, my day off! I feel like a kid in a candy store with a pocket full of pennies! There is only bad news from the war, however. My parents in Sydney are worried about us and we are worried about them. Letters take forever to get through and phones don't always work. I cannot use the phones at work, of course. Petrol is scarce, and besides Rick needs the car, so driving to see Mum and Dad is out of the question. So I will be good: clean the house and fix a nice supper. Rick will be surprised. Time to leave the typewriter and grab the broom.

3/2/42 My day off was kind of a bust. I cleaned, read, and cooked spaghetti, which Rick usually loves. He must have some Italian blood in him from way back. Rick, however, was late again and almost too tired to eat. Then he fell asleep at the table! BUT, he has been promised a day off, on March 9th, same day as my next! YEAH! We figure it's the beach, come rain or shine!

3/4/42 Terrible news: The Japanese bombed Broome in Western Australia yesterday. They did a lot of damage at the airport and the harbor. Will our airport be next? I wish Rick worked somewhere else.

3/7/42 ComCen is a madhouse, but I have made some close friends with the women I work beside. Several have kids and you can just guess the problems they have. In the time I have been there they have nearly doubled the staff. Life at home is eat and sleep. Rick seems to have a lot on his mind, but like me, he can't share it. Oh, stuff about school we talk about, no problem discussing that. He said that the Japanese children have been placed in "Protective Schooling," whatever that means. We feel sorry for them. The rest are learning current events related to the war in our area, as well as in Europe; history in the making. Rick was once a world traveler, so he is able to flesh-out the news for the students, and the kids love him.

After school, after 3PM, he is at the airport, and I think a lot more goes on there than maintaining airplanes. Whatever it is, he says that I am safer not knowing. Me, being the curious creature that I am, IT KILLS ME! Maybe I should not be even typing this. Well, day after tomorrow we get to play at the beach which is an easy bike ride, mostly down hill. We will use the two-rider we received as our wedding gift from Dad. I can't wait!

3/9/42 The war could wait! It was OUR day! We were on the road at daybreak, me in front, Rick behind. He is tall so I don't block his vision. The air this morning was so fresh and cool and not a cloud in the sky. Our home, just a cottage, is in the western subs and the beach is about six km. away. As cities go, Melbourne is nice, but reaching the country is so much nicer. Being a weekday, the beach park area was almost deserted. There were several mothers, or nannies, with kids. No lifeguards at this hour. Plenty of gulls cleaning yesterday's food scraps. The war was far away.

We padlocked the bike in the stand and walked down the path to stake our claim on a patch of sand that would become shaded later in the day. We stowed the picnic lunch under a bush and covered it with a wet towel, before rushing out to walk barefoot in the surf. The water was icy – would we really want to swim later? Now, strolling hand in hand, the stress of the recent weeks began to fade away and we began to talk. We were lovers again.

We were dressed for water, swimsuits under our clothes, so we slipped off our things and sunned until beads of sweat were beginning to roll down our arms. Suddenly, Rick snapped me up in his arms and rushed pell-mell into the water, so just as suddenly, we were completely soaked. It was like swimming in champagne, although, of course, I've never done that. It was glorious. We swam and swam, keeping a lookout for sharks and jellyfish, until finally we stumbled exhausted back to our blanket. Then the sun was our friend.

We had repeated this cycle of getting wet and drying under the sun throughout the morning, and were now eating our lunch under the shade, (by now the shade was very welcome), when a British Land Rover ground to a halt beside our bike and an Australian soldier wearing corporal stripes jumped out and ran to where we were sitting. Standing very straight and saluting, he said, "Captain Billings, Sir, I have a message from

General Nash. You are to report to him immediately and I am to provide transport. I am so sorry Ma'am, to disturb your holiday like this Ma'am" The corporal was "sorry" – I was dumbfounded! SINCE WHEN WAS RICK IN THE MILITARY? And a CAPTAIN, no less! I was rapidly growing furious!

Rick's response was a weak salute and a rumbling, "Damn, damn, damn! Can't I even have one day off? Sorry about this Mattie"

"Sorry, Sir" mumbled the soldier. "Can I take you to your home Ma'am?"

It took me a moment, but I managed to stammer, "No thanks. I'll ride the bike". Maybe by the time I got home I would simmer down – then again, maybe I would remain angry the rest of my damn life! Rick a Captain and he couldn't tell me that, not even THAT! Rick had grabbed our things and unlocked the bike without speaking. There was nothing to say. I would have bitten his head off! I rode off toward home and never looked back. I suppose the Land Rover must have passed me, but I barely could see the road ahead through my tears.

3/15/42 I have neglected my record keeping. Between sunburn and my anger at Rick's betrayal, I had a miserable few days at work and even worse at home. All I got from Rick was a phone message expressing his sorrow at spoiling my holiday and that he had to be away for a few days. He seemed clueless about why I was mad. My husband and lover: I thought I knew him, but suddenly he has become some stranger, a Captain Billings. Hides his uniform at the office, I guess. Mustn't let the "little woman" find out. She talks too much. She can't keep a lid on it. God, how those nasty thoughts kept haunting my brain.

Well, like all storms end eventually, my anger did too. Five days later Rick was waiting for me when I walked out of ComCen. There he stood, all smiles, dressed in his airfield coveralls (no uniform or Captain's bars). He was hoping to take me out to dinner, and he held a bunch of flowers in his hand. He needed a good slap in the face, but I kissed him instead. I kissed him and hugged him until one of my office friends stepped up and said, "Hey! I thought you two were married! You act like yer engaged. Hey, hey hey!"

So, we went out to eat. His coveralls were not that clean and I looked a bit frayed at the edges, but we dined out anyway at a little bar with great seafood and beer. We got a quiet spot in a corner, so I, very lovingly, asked him what the hell he was up to. Well, Rick has a smile that can melt an iceberg, which he turned on, and simply murmured, "Later." So, we held hands and enjoyed good food, but the real conversation came later, back at home.

The moment the door clicked shut he took me in his arms and kissed me. It was a real one! Then we settled on the couch and he let out a big sigh. This appeared to be so difficult for him, like he was confessing a sin. Finally he began, "This morning I got a moment alone with Nash and explained how my driver blew my cover inadvertently so I needed his permission to tell you something about what was going on. It may put you in some personal danger, but here is what I am now allowed to say: I am currently an undercover agent in the Air Force of the United States, Captain rank. I hope to heaven you have not told anyone, even your mother or father what you heard. Believe me, I chewed out the driver when I had him alone! I think he knew better, but it slipped out. I'll bet you were surprised to hear him call me that, and even

35

saluting. But spoiling our picnic, what a crime! You didn't tell anyone did you?"

The guy still didn't get it! "No, I kept it to myself, Dear." I replied. (Kept it to myself and burned like the fires of hell for five days!) The way men think!

Then he continued, "I have been put on leave from teaching at the academy, presumably to spend full time repairing aircraft, which is my cover for what I am really doing now days. But that is top secret. So tell your friends I come home greasy every night from maintaining birds at the airport – OK?"

"Soooo, that's the story, is it?" I replied, "The whole truth and nothing but the truth. Well, it is an improvement over what I was imagining. Oh honey I was feeling downright murderous, I felt deceived, which I DAMN WELL was, and you have acted as if I was all huffy about the picnic and pumping that two-rider up the hills by myself. Well, it was a bit hard, but that wasn't why I was mad. I guess I should have been mad at that General Nash for making you deceive me. Oh honey, I love you so much."

Well, that is all I will write about that evening, except that it was truly lovely and very intimate.

3/17/42 More bad news: Japanese have moved into the Solomon Islands and there is word they have an air base on Guadalcanal. This is on the radio, but what I hear at ComCen would make your hair stand on end! That's all I dare write.

Our married life, well that is going just fine, especially since I now know more about the man I am married to. Now I feel I have a part of the action, so to speak. When he can't talk I know why. I'm part of the team.

3/18/42 A bunch of drunks murdered that Japanese gardener at the market. He was an innocent victim, as nice a man as you could find, an Australian citizen I'm told. I feel so sorry for him and his family. People get so crazy! I will send them flowers if I can find out where they live.

3/20/42 Rick brought a friend home for supper. Rick explained to me that this guy was between girlfriends, craving friendship, and needed to be fattened up. I decided it would be steaks on the grill out on the deck. His name is Bill Andrews, "Andy" for short. He smokes so I banned him from the house; on the deck it kept the bugs away! "So what do you do, Andy?" I asked.

"Me? Oh I keep the radios working down at the airport. Rick services engines and I do radios. Rick gets greasier than I do, but we're both very busy these days," he said. He was giving me a knowing look and I got the message – another man with a secret life.

After supper and a couple of beers, the guys wandered off to "inspect the vegetable garden" and spent nearly an hour down there quietly talking, not about veggies I am sure! But I did not mind since I was now a silent partner, part of a team. And I had my secrets too at ComCen, things I kept from Rick. I went inside, found some nice music on the radio and settled down with my book.

I did not get far in my book, when the music was interrupted by a news bulletin: US General MacArthur left the Philippines and was here in Australia, ordered here by President Roosevelt. The Japanese have a death grip on Luzon. It is old news for me, since I work at ComCen, but now I can write it here. I have to be so careful.

3/21/42 I am free today, my day off. Tomorrow I begin evening shift for a month, so really it is like two days off. Then I got the surprise of my life: Rick came home about 9 AM, came bounding in the house, took me in his arms, kissed me passionately, and said, "I have to be away for a few days." What a let down! I thought he had something else in mind! "Andy will be with me," he said, as if that made a difference.

"When did you decide to do this?" I said.

"Nash makes my decisions for me; you know that. He told us half an hour ago and my plane is warming up now. We are to take off ASAP. I can't tell you what is up, but maybe you will find out at ComCen. I love you Honey, but I got to grab a couple things and go. Andy is already there I think."

So I replied, "Sounds like this guy, Andy, is more important than me." It was meant as a joke, but it came across all wrong. "I'm sorry, I didn't mean that, Rick," I said, but he had already left the room. Minutes later, after proper goodbyes, Rick roared off with his army corporal, leaving our car for me. I had two days to kill and no husband to kill them with. Well, the garden did need weeding.

4/24/42 Look at that date! Rick has been gone a whole month, and yes I am worried sick. Working the evening shift at ComCen at least gives my mind something else to think about, although the thoughts are far from pleasant. One exception: US General Jimmy Doolittle "out-did" himself and pulled off an air raid on the Japanese homeland. He gave them a taste of their own medicine! But, then again, how many innocent women and children died too? There is no such thing as a good act of war.

To make the time go easier, I am doing daycare for about ten children, preschoolers, whose parents are working. It leaves me little time for this record, but there is little to say. When I start to write, I start to cry, so I scrap it. Rick was wrong about my hearing something about what he and Andy are doing, were doing, from ComCen. I have left messages with

General Nash's secretary but no response. So a few days has become a month. Will it become a year? Forever? I mustn't think such thoughts.

4/25/42 I got a call from General Nash. Rick's plane was forced down, no mention where, but the general has "good reason to believe that Rick was able to bale out to safety". He could not elaborate, he explained, for security reasons. I thanked him for his information, but realized that I was being fed a lot of pabulum. He didn't know any more than I did, but it made my mind relax a little.

4/26/42 I find I like the night shift at work. I have one friend at ComCen, Barb, whose husband is in combat up north somewhere. She has a great sense of humor and we keep each other laughing. That's better than crying, although we do that too. She lives just down the road, no children, but she has two huge dogs her husband bought her for safety. She keeps them well fed, thank goodness!

Since we both work there at ComCen we do share secrets and today she told me something that does give me hope, but I cannot write it here. I hope to find out more soon. Maybe I should not have been so harsh about Nash's comment: Maybe there was good news and he did not dare tell me. Sometimes this security thing drives me nuts.

5/25/43 I am back on the day shift. It's the days off that get to me the most. Mum and Dad came down for two weeks to cheer me up. Lot of good that did! Mum can't help tearing up and all Dad talks about is how Rick "was" such a hero, as if he's dead for sure. My friend, Barb is better at it; she cracks jokes. Mum heard her once and was offended and said I should be too. Oh well, you can't please everyone.

6/16/42 It has been raw and chill and our furnace is acting strange. As soon as Barb heard about it she insisted that I live with her, at least for a while. She has a potbelly stove in her living room. That works almost too well. We play games and read the books on her shelf. (She has the sexiest novels.) If there is a good picture show at the Ritz, we go see it. We keep the radio off for the most part – no sense making ourselves blue. There's been nothing much to write about.

9/6/42 Finally, some good news! Japanese marines attacked the Royal Australian Air Force base at Milne Bay and we soundly beat them back. Who says we can't lick those rascals. No word about my Rick however.

CHAPTER THREE
RECOLLECTIONS BY ANDY

My name is William Andrews. New friends call me Bill, but my service buddies, back then, called me Andy. At the time of this story, I was a lowly corporal in the Australian Army. I was, nevertheless, the electronics brain of my outfit. My rank had little to do with my experience. Before the war, I was an electrical engineering student, and had worked at the radio repair shop at Melbourne Airport during school breaks for over a year.

When war began to look inevitable, I joined the Australian Army. Being a bit on the clumsy side, I fouled up basic training on the range by firing at the wrong target. With that on my record, I was lucky to make corporal! Then the Army took over the airfield as a base and I got my old job back in the radio shop. That's where I met Billings. Rick was an undercover US Army officer, a captain, and he chose me to be his mate on the mission I will relate here. Many years have past, but I recall the events vividly. It is now declassified, so I shall tell it as I recall it. I invite my reader to travel back with me to those heady days.

There are some dates that I never forget. March 22, 1942 is one of them. That was the morning we took off from Melbourne, extra fuel tanks weighing us down, heading right toward enemy territory. We were given a single engine Cessna with civilian markings and, of course, we wore civilian flying gear. We also had a flimsy cover story in case we were captured.

Our destination was Mount Wilhelm in Papua, New Guinea. The plan called for us to arrive in the evening. There would be no moon, but there might be cloud cover. Cloud cover was a big concern. It would help to hide us, but it could obscure our target, even cause us to crash. There, as high as possible on the eastern slope, we were to airdrop a transponder with its battery pack, and hope to heaven it survived the landing. There was a small black parachute to break the fall, but this device used delicate vacuum tubes. Those tough little transistors had not been invented yet. So, if a tube didn't break, if we didn't crash into the mountain, and if the Japanese didn't shoot us down, and if the engine didn't run out of fuel, we might make it back to Australia and be heroes. Frankly, the odds were not that great.

So, why were we doing this? Our forces, both naval and air, needed a third point, a radio contact point, to aid in navigating the Solomon Islands. They had reliable stations on New Caledonia and Australia, but Papua New Guinea was largely occupied by the enemy and they had destroyed our station. The coordinates of Mount Wilhelm are well documented, so a station placed there was the answer. Why a transponder? A transponder only sends a signal in response to a secret frequency broadcast by one of our ships or planes needing a fix. Without that signal triggering it, the transponder remains quiet and undetected.

The first leg was easy enough, to Cape York Peninsula, Australia, with several stops along the way. The plane was typical of what a bush pilot might fly; good fuel mileage at slow speed. Using a fighter plane, they said, would attract too much attention, but if the Japanese did spot us, we were at their mercy. Hopefully, they would think we were not worth the trouble. The best plan, we felt, was to fly low, close to the treetops.

The airstrip at the Cape was recently lengthened to accommodate large aircraft. The old hanger sat unoccupied since it was an obvious target, everything of importance had been moved to tents under trees. An ach-ach battery was at the ready. There was a sense of anticipation, almost electric, in the air and on the faces of the men we met. The war was growing close!

We were briefed again about our mission, this time with contour maps of Papua and suggested route following river valleys. That evening we were given a fine meal in the officer's mess and allowed to sleep until late the following morning. Take-off was planned for early afternoon so we would reach our target a bit after sunset giving us some light to see by. We were to make our drop, then fly around the peak to the west side and head home by a new route. We were only to break radio silence when we were over water on our return. It sounded simple enough.

Well, the meal was delicious and the beer was cold, but the conversation had a depressing undercurrent. The US General Douglas MacArthur, they said, had just arrived in Australia, having been forced to leave the Philippines, where things were going very badly. The Japanese had made far more progress than I had realized. They had seized most of the ports on Papua, many of which had little or no defenses. The interior of the island, much of it unexplored, was a different matter. Here native tribes held sway. Rumor had it that some tribes still practiced headhunting, so the average white adventurer stayed near the edges of the island. The very idea of your head mounted on a bamboo pole as a war trophy was not a pretty picture! Thus the interior remained mostly unexplored.

The Solomon Islands to the east were also in serious danger. Our precious transponder was vital for our forces and I felt the pressure of our mission. So, despite the fact that our cots that night had real mattresses and pillows, I slept very little. Rick did better. He snored all night long! I must have slept some, however, because at 1100 hours I was rudely shaken awake by Rick, saying something like, "Hey man! You going to sleep all day too?" There was a lot I could have responded, but I kept my mouth shut.

We lifted off at 1300 hours in clear weather. Over the water I would have preferred some cloud cover. We felt quite vulnerable with no place to hide. We went over the yarn we were to tell the Japanese, in the event of our capture, about trying to rescue a pair of explorers in trouble. By the time we made land we almost believed our own story. We felt safer now, flying low over the trees. By doing this we were vulnerable to small arms fire and, of course, a miscalculation on our part, but when a plane flies low and fast those on the ground have little time to react. I was glad then that Rick had enjoyed a good nights sleep and was a superb pilot.

After about an hour of this hair-raising flying, Rick brought the plane up to a safer altitude. We were far inland now and heading north-northeast for Mount Wilhelm. We had seen nothing of the enemy so far and assumed we were safe this far inland. Besides that, cloud cover had increased, making ground hopping extremely dangerous. Mount Wilhelm is tall, 4509 meters, but maybe not tall enough to stand above the clouds. If it came into view, we would stay above the clouds, make our drop and scoot for home. I watched the sea of clouds with the binoculars until my eyes burned, but no mountaintop appeared.

It was almost sunset, very pretty over the clouds, but not what we wanted to see. If all the calculations had been correct, we should be almost there. I saw only two choices: Fail in our mission or drop below the clouds and hope to find our way. Then Rick had a better idea: Fly east until we were over the ocean, drop down near the water, turn west to find the coast, locate the Romu River, follow it for about 250km (about 150 miles), then veer off due west to our target. Great way to become heroes! We would be close to Wewak and Madang where the Japanese would find us an easy target. So I said, "Great idea! Let's go!"

It worked surprisingly well, up to a point. We found the ocean under the clouds, swung west, found what had to be the Romu River, followed it for a while before trouble hit. I think it was the surprise element that got us that far. We were the last thing the Japanese expected; a little private plane whizzing through like a mosquito.

Then things went wrong, and fast! Rick had enough room between the treetops and the clouds, but we had to climb fast to avoid crashing into a hillside, which slowed us enough for the men on the ground to grab their rifles and do considerable damage. I believe they hit a fuel line or wire, because the engine stopped. Rick then switched tanks and got the engine going again, and for a few seconds we were doing OK. I was watching the gauges so Rick could concentrate on flying. The needle on tank-2 caught my attention. It was spinning wildly downward; the tank had been torn open and would be empty in no time! We were roaring down a sort of wide canyon, when Rick ordered me to jump. Well, when a captain tells a corporal to jump, he jumps! I jumped! And I pulled my cord at the same instant, fearing I might hit the ground before it unfurled. Apparently Rick had considered that too, climbing as quickly as possible. When I landed it was only as if I had jumped off a high stool. I was pretty happy until I looked around and found myself surrounded by soldiers, some with fixed bayonets! I had no weapon and I had a three-day growth of beard and I wore bush clothes (I was a "civilian," remember?) so I just raised my hands as high as I could and let them capture me.

It was a minute later that I heard the muffled sound of the plane crash. I had been trying to see if Rick's chute opened, praying to see it, but I never did. Rick was a superb pilot, so he might have survived the crash. I've heard of pilots who at the last second, steered between two trees, ripping off the wings, but saving their life. Rick was that kind of pilot, at least I hoped so!

I was given little time to think about Rick however. After being frisked, I was taken, with a bayonet poking my back, to see their company commander. He was a short squat man wearing thick glasses and an expression that warned me to choose my words carefully. He studied me all over as if I were some new biological specimen. Finally he settled behind a desk and indicated that I might sit as well. I was not handcuffed, but there was a soldier on each side of me.

Speaking English he said, "State your name, rank and serial number, and your reason for being here."

I replied, "My name is William A. Andrews. The A stands for Abel, spelled a-b-e-l. I am not in the military, Sir. I work for a small Australian company called Outback Adventures.

Two of our clients have become stranded due to the hostilities and we planned to drop them food and clothing."

He was now studying my phony business ID, intentionally aged, and the other contents of my wallet. They had emptied my pockets, even taking my cigarettes. Finally he spoke, "These clients you speak of, where did you expect to find them? Did you have some place to rendezvous? I presume you had radio contact. Tell me about these people, what they were up to."

So I gave him the story we had contrived about a man and wife anthropologist team, there to study the local tribes. I said we were to find a small clearing with a large stone cross about 30 km west of the Ramu River, and about 350 km from where the Ramu meets the ocean.

He sat for some time, apparently weighing my story, giving it time to sink in. Finally he straightened up in his chair and said, "Good story, but we both know you are lying, now don't we? Put him in Number Three, Sergeant". The last words were in Japanese. (I understood Japanese, but I intended to keep this knowledge secret).

"Number Three" it turned out was a crude stockade, about 4m high, topped with razor wire. Sitting under shade, machine guns at the ready, sat two soldiers watching the corners. The moment the gate closed behind me, I was surrounded by anxious faces, seeking news I might have – any news. I had little to give, except to repeat what I had said before. They had seen our plane, the engine coughing and sputtering, and seen me leave the plane and my chute open. After that the fence hid their view.

Now I had a chance to study my surroundings, before the daylight failed entirely. Most of the prisoners were men, but there were a few women and about ten or so children. An older man with a distinguished manner approached me and introduced himself as Bernmeister, formally the village mayor. He was Dutch by ancestry he told me proudly. It seemed that he enjoyed the respect of the other prisoners. He explained the rules to me. He pointed out that along one wall was a slit trench. "Don't fall in!" he said with a faint smile. Next to the gate sat a pail of water and a dipper, ONLY to be used for drinking. They had already been fed, so I probably would not get food until the next morning. Lowering his voice, he said, "The food is terrible, but if you can't stomach it, give it someone else. We are all starving!" Then he continued, "The worst however is the rain. Numbers One and Two have a thatch roof over them, but we must squat in the rain or bake in the sun. If we ask for a roof they laugh at us. Well, now the ground is dry so try to get some sleep, my friend."

Sleep sounded like a good idea, but where? It appeared that every inch was taken until I spotted two men with their arms and legs sprawled out, using more room than necessary so I approached them warily. I asked them politely in English, coupled with hand signs if I might sleep between them. They sat up immediately and began to bargain for the space privileges. My hat and my leather flight jacket would satisfy them. I indicated that their price was much too high, and was moving away when Bernmeister motioned me to his corner. There close beside him lay his wife and snuggled in her arms, a little girl, perhaps three or four years of age. All he said was, "Sleep next to me. I'll introduce you to my wife and little one in the morning." So, lying on my back, in the dirt next to my benefactor, hat for a pillow, I managed to get some sleep, but it was sleep filled with nightmares about Rick's fate.

The days and weeks that followed were tedious and despite an early attempt at marking off the days, I finally abandoned the effort, completely losing track of time. We were fed twice a day and it was indeed very poor. I found one Australian who became a friend and chess playing companion, (he had devised a crude board), but I did not trust him, or anyone else, with the true reason for our mission. Bernmeister was the voice of reason in the stockade, settling arguments, dispensing justice, and occasionally making deals with the Japanese. Once a Japanese colonel inspected our stockade and to everyone's surprise, the following day a crew of native builders began work on a large bamboo and thatch roof over our entire area! We all assumed that Bernmeister had somehow pulled off this miracle, but he claimed not. His comment, "Not all Japs are bad."

One morning several months after my capture, I was shackled and taken to the company commander. This time there were several other officers in the room. Again I was asked to explain my presence in Papua, and again I told my story. Now, with the CO translating for me, I was asked even more questions. Obviously I was now "a person of interest." I was returned to the stockade for the day, but the following morning, shackled again and marched off with a platoon of soldiers in the general direction of the Ramu River. They are calling my bluff, I thought. They want to capture my "clients." It would be a long walk indeed!

Soon we picked up a well-worn trail running close to the river on the west side. It was tiresome walking with my hands behind my back, so when we stopped to rest at an old campsite by the river, I asked the sergeant if my arms could be freed. He thought about it, then asked the lieutenant, who also thought about it. It was a big decision apparently. Finally the sergeant came to me, turned me about and removed my bindings. As he did so he said, "You run, we shoot." What a relief to have my arms free! I could now stand naturally and was even permitted to step into the cool water and wash my face. The rest stop was all too short however. A bark from the lieutenant and we were on our way again. The path led us away from the river now, climbing steadily to higher ground. Here the air was fresher, and since I could now swing my arms, I was beginning to find the march quite tolerable.

Suddenly the stillness of the jungle was broken by a rifle shot and looking up I got a glimpse of a tall native tribesman, disappear from sight, apparently wounded! "Head hunters, head hunters!" the soldiers were saying in Japanese. There were also words I picked up about poison arrows. The soldiers were clearly frightened; this was something they were not prepared for. All forward motion had stopped. The man guarding me moved behind a tree leaving me as a suitable target for arrows, but none came. In fact, no more natives appeared at all.

Finally, the lieutenant barked an order and we were moving again, faster than before. Before long we came to a native village, recently deserted, it appeared, since a cook fire was still burning. I think the soldiers were fearful of an ambush however, because within minutes we were leaving on another path in a southwesterly direction. The idea it seemed was to get as far from the natives as possible! To me, an Australian, with some knowledge of the many tribes of New Guinea, the idea of headhunters among them seemed almost laughable. How rumors persist! The practice had ended, or so I'd been told, except on the island of Borneo.

The trail here was apparently less traveled and treacherous under foot. By my estimate we had hiked at least 40km since morning, and the murmured curses of the soldiers meant it was well past time to bivouac for the night. Finally the lieutenant called a halt and we settled down. I was given one of their field rations and a canteen of water, all-in-all a very tasty meal. I was sitting comfortably leaning against a small tree, enjoying the last bits of my field rations, when the lieutenant came by to check on me. This is when I made a really dumb mistake: I did not jump to my feet and stand at attention. Instead, I slowly rose to my feet – much too slowly! To the lieutenant I was insulting his rank and, too late, I saw the fury rising in his face. I stood now, backed against the tree, as he shouted insults at me, ending with orders to tie my arms behind the tree. Thus began the most miserable night of my life. The soldier assigned to guard me was now afraid to free me even to relieve myself. I shall not elaborate further. It was a terrible night!

When daybreak finally came and I was untied, I sensed a sort of camaraderie with some of the soldiers. I had "paid my dues" and gained their respect. One man even gave me a drag on the cigarette he was smoking! After another field ration, we were expecting the order to move out, but instead, the lieutenant began sending scouts out in different directions. When he came over to me I stood stiffly at attention and he greeted me with a smile. He asked me what type of airplane we had been flying, who else was on board, what was on board, and the markings on the craft. I answered each question with a "Sir". Seemingly pleased with my answers, he put me at ease, offered me a cigarette and lighted it for me with a lighter! Quite a change from the night before! Then he explained in a confidential tone that he expected to locate the wreckage in this area, and the craft's contents would be "most interesting." Yes indeed, I thought!

Well, this was a restful day, and I certainly needed one. I sat under a tree, my young guardian across from me, rifle pointed in my direction. One other soldier, apparently ill, sat some distance away. All the others, even the lieutenant, had left in pairs to search for our plane. It was a peaceful scene, quiet, except for the jungle sounds, which were anything but quiet. It gave me time to think. Why, I thought, why would the Japanese devote so much manpower, time and energy to locate a downed civilian plane, unless they were onto our true mission? If the transponder was found, I was prepared to tell them, that it was for our clients so we could locate them in the future. (Our phony company logo had been stenciled to the side for just this contingency). It was clear now that it was the plane, not the "clients" that they were seeking. They knew that I had lied. Had I been so very transparent in my storytelling? My eyes perhaps, maybe they gave me away. As a boy, my mother always knew instantly when I attempted a lie. Then, of course, there was the other troubling thought: Maybe Rick would be found in the wreckage! I wracked my brain, but no other explanation for this trek in the jungle made sense.

By mid-afternoon, men began returning; one with an exciting yarn to tell about his encounter with a wild boar, but no crumpled Cessna had yet been found. The lieutenant and his companion were the last to return, anger and disappointment written all over his face. He was looking for someone to blame. He grilled the men about what they had seen and insulted them for not seeing more. He seemed not to care if the men hated him or not. I understood everything I heard, but pretended not to listen. Finally, without having eaten and despite encroaching darkness, he gave the order to march on! There was muttered swearing, but everyone shouldered his gear and marched on. It was rocky underfoot and hard to see where to step. We must have gone several kilometers when the lieutenant himself tripped and fell, and unless the man was deaf, he heard the laughter and it must have stung. Getting to his feet he screamed the order to bivouac. I almost felt pity for the man. Clearly his men disliked him. He was probably intelligent, but was falling prey to his own demons!

That night I was allowed to sleep unbound, but guarded. The weather had been dry until now, but during the night it began to rain. The soldiers all put on their ponchos, which, if they squatted, kept them quite dry. I wore my soft leather Aussie hat, it's wide brim providing some protection. The sergeant, however, had appropriated my leather flight jacket. Who was I to object? Soon I was quite wet, but since there was little air stirring, I managed to keep warm enough. I squatted under a tree, and I may have dozed off a little. Still, it was a big improvement over the night before.

The next morning the lieutenant reappeared as a calm and friendly fellow. He came over to me, put me at ease and told me he had found the flaw in the intelligence he had been given previously. The place to search is a few kilometers further on this trail and in the jungle to the right. Now he was certain he said. Why was he telling me these things? He seemed to need someone to impress since he realized that he had lost the confidence of his men. He was a pathetic soul indeed.

We lost no time in resuming the march and by late morning the lieutenant had us stop at the new search location. We were at the edge of a beautiful mountain meadow, nearly treeless, and covered with wild flowers. The rain had stopped and the brilliant sun shinning on the wet flowers created a scene that reminded me of paintings by the French masters. In the distance off to the southwest, rose Mount Wilhelm in the cloudless sky. It was a lovely panorama, but possibly dangerous. No soldier wants to be that exposed.

The lieutenant and his sergeant were conferring now over a field map, and studying the forest on the other side of the meadow with binoculars. Now it was the sergeant who turned to us and gave the orders: We were all to cross the meadow, a distance of about a kilometer, and regroup on the other side. We could spread out and find our own way across the stream that wound down the central, swampy area. Two men were to guard me.

It soon became clear that the stream was actually split up into many tiny streams flowing through a bog. That was why it was treeless. By jumping carefully from one grassy clump to the next, we could keep our feet dry, but a slip meant a soaking up to the knees. The lieutenant led the way and the sergeant took up the rear.

The lieutenant soon was far ahead of us, leaping from clump to clump. I was somewhere near the middle of the meadow when we heard the lieutenant scream and begin firing his sidearm at something in the water! He had slipped and was waist deep in water and struggling with something hidden from our view. A young corporal reached him first and began lifting him onto the embankment. As he emerged from the water we saw a large snake, perhaps a water moccasin, still attached to the man's thigh. Thinking quickly, the soldier took his trench knife and severed the snake's head from its body. The body, fully a meter long, wriggled grotesquely in its death throws and sank into the stream. The head however remained fastened and had to be pried apart! The medic was at his side now, cutting away his pants and applying a snakebite kit, attempting to pump out the venom.

We had all caught up by this time, making a wide circle around the stricken man. Suddenly the medic realized that the lieutenant had no pulse; he had gone into cardiac arrest!

The sergeant began CPR and continued for several minutes but got no response. The lieutenant, his face distorted, eyes staring, was dead. It had happened so fast!

In the hushed silence that followed, I studied the faces of the soldiers. All showed the same expression of sadness, even heartbreak. In life they had found much to dislike in this man. In death he was their comrade and they mourned their loss. But there was no time to lose; with four men to carry his body he was moved to the wooded area beyond. The platoon had no portable radio, so news of the death must wait for our return. There, at the edge of the woods, the sergeant put one man to work digging a grave while others in pairs were to complete the lieutenant's mission: to find our plane. This time I was included in the search.

Speaking now to the whole group, the sergeant explained that the wreckage had been spotted on a reconnaissance flight, about a kilometer west of the meadow. (Ah, but the meadow was easily five kilometers long!) He said we must complete the mission or die trying. (I was sure he meant it.) That night we were to regroup at the gravesite.

The jungle was thin at first, but became denser as we went deeper. The Cessna had been repainted before we left Australia. Now it was a dull gray with OUTBACK ADVENTURES stenciled on the side in green, not the easiest colors to spot in a jungle. About mid-afternoon we were surprised to hear three shots and see a red flair fired into the sky: the signal that it had been found. It was not too far from where we were so, instead of returning to the gravesite, we opted on seeing it for ourselves. All of the soldiers were equipped with compasses so with the new heading we changed direction. Of course, sighting on a flair, which we only saw after it was far above the trees and which the wind might have shifted from its vertical path was an iffy business at best. We moved cautiously, snakes and other wild creatures very much on our minds. The three of us formed a line; the lead man carried a pole in one hand and a machete in the other. I came next and the other soldier watched over us with his rifle at the ready.

In the end it was the sound of voices that lead us to the crash site. The plane had lost one wing in the treetop, which is what the reconnaissance plane had spotted. The rest of the fuselage had come to rest nose down on the jungle floor. One man stood by the wreck; the other had crawled inside. Was Rick in there too? To my relief, their conversation soon indicated that he was not. Next to come out of the plane was our "air-drop" bag, (part of our cover story), but also intended for Rick and me if we were stranded. It was a padded canvas bag, full of non-perishable food, with the phony company logo stenciled on the side. It was opened in no time and all four soldiers immediately sat down to enjoy a picnic before the sergeant reached them. Even I was given a can of cold hash to eat.

I was pleased to see the interest in the food bag since it diverted attention away from the transponder that was still in the plane, tied behind the seats. It was sure to be found, of course, eventually. They had found the carbine and ammo stashed under the seat, the two machetes we brought, the first aid kit, and a nearly full carton of my cigarettes. These were already being smoked and although I was tempted to ask for one, I did not.

They had consumed their fill of canned rations and were now going back to the plane for a more thorough search. Two men had climbed inside, one guarded me, and the forth began to inspect the engine. He was smoking one of my precious cigarettes, took one last draw, and dropped the butt to the ground. It was a serious mistake! Instantly the entire area was engulfed to flames from aircraft fuel that had soaked the jungle floor! Running wildly now, then rolling on the ground, he was badly burned before we were able to catch him and smother the flames. The men in the plane fared better. They both jumped to safety escaping the flames, but one injured his ankle, possibly a break.

It quickly became apparent that I was the only member of the group with some experience as a medic. I poured my canteen water on the burned man's skin to cool the surface and then did what I could to prevent shock. The poor man was in terrible pain. The others stood back and let me work, and I seemed to be making some progress when the man suddenly grabbed his sidearm, brought it to his temple and fired! No one spoke. We were all transfixed by the horror of the moment. The only sound was the roaring of the flames consuming the Cessna; consuming the Cessna and the transponder, and whatever else the Japanese expected to find in the wreckage. It was all being destroyed before our eyes!

I now turned my attention to the ankle patient. The ankle was swollen, but apparently not broken. I fixed him up with sort of a walking splint and one of the men made him a crutch. Our next concern was fear that the forest might catch fire, and it might have if the men had not beat it out as the fire died down. There was nothing to be done now but watch the fire die down and wait for the sergeant to find us. Perhaps he had not seen the flair; yet the three shots must have been heard. Where was he?

We had been told, however, to regroup at the lieutenant's gravesite around dusk, so it was time to start back. Using field shovels, we dug a firebreak around the plane's charred remains, and prepared to leave. Using a makeshift litter for the dead man that I helped carry, our pathetic little party returned to the gravesite to spend the night. We were last to arrive and when the sergeant heard our story he simply sat there staring at the ground. Their mission had been a failure on nearly every count. What would he tell his commander when we returned?

The following morning, the sergeant had an answer to that question: a carefully contrived lie. He brought us all together and explained that if the truth got out about what really happened yesterday, we were all in very serious trouble with the commander. The revised story of events was to be as follows: FIRST- The lieutenant's death would be just as it occurred except that the burned man was first to rush to the lieutenant's aid, and he too was bitten, by a second snake. He was a real hero deserving a medal for devotion to duty. The medic did his best, but both men died within seconds. SECOND- When the plane was found it was a burned wreck, having burned on impact. THIRD- Everything found on the plane, even including the carbine and my carton of cigarettes was to be buried with the men and forgotten! Then he looked directly at me and said, "The same goes for you. One word out of place and you are a dead man!" I believed he meant it. Then speaking more softly, he added "Thank you for doing your best to help these clowns. You are the only one with brains." Then he walked away and presided over the burial of two men and the gear from the plane.

When the pit was partly filled he came to me and said, "Come, take me to the plane. I want to see it for myself." It took about an hour to get there and as we walked he surprised me by revealing the real reason the commander was so interested in our plane. Upon the Japanese capture of Lae, on the coast south of us, they had destroyed the radio signal station used by Australian and American forces for navigation. It was of vital importance, especially to the Americans who were unfamiliar with this part of the world, so it was logical that a new replacement station of some kind be established. The commander reasoned that an American invention, the transponder, might be placed on Mount Wilhelm, or some similar location with known coordinates. And perhaps, he reasoned, Outback Adventures might have had that mission. (The commander had read me like a book!) The sergeant glanced over at me to observe my reaction. I said the logic was interesting, but did not apply to our mission.

"Well anyway," he said, "He wants to get his hands on a transponder in the worst way. He wants to send one to Tokyo for our engineers to study. That would get him a promotion for sure. Our whole mission was to get that bastard a higher rank. He won't be happy now, and I am certain to lose my stripes. Luck of the draw."

Aircraft fuel fires leave a very distinctive odor. We smelled this one long before our arrival at the wreck. Anything with any weight had fallen out of the craft to the ground. The remains of the transponder, since it was heavy, probably lay at the bottom of the heap, well hidden by other debris. I prayed that it might stay there. Fortunately the sergeant did not seem inclined to dirty his clothes in the mess. He just needed to tell the commander that he had been to the site and seen nothing that resembled a transponder. "I wonder what happened to your friend. Maybe we will have a surprise and find him along the way." he said, "I've seen enough here. Let's go."

Those words, spoken so casually by the sergeant, summarized my own private thoughts during this entire mission. I had been searching the jungle as best I could for some sign, some clue to Rick's whereabouts. He had to be out there somewhere near our route, dead or alive. We had only seen one native village, indicating that this territory was their domain, their hunting ground. Might they not have found him and sheltered him? When we entered that compound, I seemed almost to feel his presence, but, actually to my relief, we moved on.

It is interesting how some memories come back so strongly, and other fade into the mists of time. As I look back over the years, I can barely recall our return to the Japanese camp. I do recall how carefully we skirted around that native village of "headhunters." It struck me as quite funny at the time, but these soldiers were not taking any changes. If I had suffered the loss of two of my comrades-in-arms, I suppose I might have shared their fear. I remember that the soldier with the bruised ankle was soon walking normally and I was rewarded for my services by his glowing report to the commander. I was given VIP quarters in a wooden building with a cot to sleep on! At times I was employed as a company doctor, still under guard of course. I considered trying to escape, but realized I had no place to escape to.

About mid-September, all hell broke loose in the air over Wewak, just north of our camp. The Japanese had a major air base there and American planes caught them off guard. I could see some of the action from my quarters. Days later, I was able to discuss it with my old friend, Bernmeister, the mayor, who always had his ear to the ground. (Our captors, perhaps sensing that one day the tables might be turned, had moved the mayor and his family to a building like mine, including occasional visiting privileges.) From him I learned that the strike was a major victory for our Allied forces, one we badly needed, perhaps even a turning point in the war. Together we had a quiet celebration.

In the end, about a year later, the tables had indeed turned. The Allies occupied the coastal towns of Wewak, Madang, and Lae. Soon, in a scene that can best be described as glorious chaos, we were greeted by American forces and set free. I got the ear of a US Marine major and explained that a Captain Richard Billings was probably languishing in a native village not too far away and should be rescued as well. He said, "We'll look into it," and told me to join a group boarding a Liberty Ship bound for Sydney. I saluted and got in line.

After returning to my beloved Australia I was debriefed about the mission we had been on and again pleaded the case for Rick's rescue. Again I got a, "We'll look into it" and was dismissed. I got a new uniform and a week of R&R in Sydney, before returning to Melbourne where I was to report to General Nash for assignment.

Had I done all I could to help Rick? I did not feel confident that anyone had really heard me. Corporals don't tell majors what to do. I wandered down to the airport and managed to find a free ride to Melbourne. Then would come the biggest test of courage I had ever faced: I would visit Mattie Billings!

CHAPTER FOUR
MATTIE'S DIARY

9/14/42 This is my day off. This morning I got a phone call from General Nash inviting me to lunch. His driver would pick me up at 11:30. He sort of indicated that he had good news for me. Naturally I said "yes," saluted the phone, and prettied myself up. The driver arrived at 11:30 on the dot. I sort of expected to see the general in the car, but the driver said he would be waiting at the restaurant. He was not a talkative sort so I didn't ask any more questions.

Well, I expected the restaurant would be upscale, but the place we came to was a palace overlooking the ocean, and posh with formal gardens, now winterized. We entered at a side entrance (that should have told me something), up an elevator, and down a hall to a door. The driver gave three light taps and I heard the door being unlocked on the inside. I began to feel very uneasy! This was no luncheon engagement. This was a trap, and I was sure of it when the general relocked the door after I entered!

"May I take your coat?" he said. I felt like saying, "NO" and running for my life, but I didn't. I looked about the room.

A table for two was set by the window with wine glasses and a bottle on ice." I hope you like Bordeaux," he said.

Finally I got my vocal chords working and said, "Can you tell me anything about my husband? It has been months and it is driving me crazy!"

"Now, now relax Mattie. I want to find Rick as much as you do. I can tell you this: His mission was in Papua and his plane went down. His route was not over enemy territory, not much anyway, so I am sure the men jumped to safety. They are probably dining on coconuts right now," he said with a smirk. (God, how I wanted to wipe that smile off his face!) Instead I said nothing. I pretended to be interested in the pictures on the wall. He came up behind and put a hand on my shoulder. I removed it! He pulled out my chair and I sat down. He poured the wine and I took a sip. I could feel something rising within me – a tsunami of emotion, powerful, irrepressible. I gripped my teeth together!

He studied me from the other side of the table. "You are very quiet," he said "I get the feeling you don't trust me. I was hoping we could get better acquainted, that is all. You are a very beautiful woman you know and I like to talk to beautiful women. Is that a crime?"

"No" I replied, "But seducing your employees is. You wouldn't be doing that, now would you General Nash? This is a nice apartment. I bet you have a king size bed in the next room. How many women troop through here in a month? Does your wife know about this apartment? I have met Nancy, you know, I baby sit for her. Small world isn't it General?" I was burning my bridges, but somehow the rage I was feeling was burning out of control. I was hanging the man on purely circumstantial evidence. I was out of control and couldn't stop myself!

Suddenly we were both standing, glaring at each other. The general's face was rapidly growing red and there was a menacing expression in his eyes. "You ungrateful little bitch," he murmured, "You need to be taught a lesson." Stepping from behind the table, he suddenly grabbed my wrist and twisted my arm behind my back, simultaneously slamming his napkin hard against my mouth with his other hand. I was trapped, but it had happened too fast for fear to set in. My hand found the nearly full wineglass on the table and with all the strength I could muster, I slammed it into his face. I apparently did some damage, because he relinquished his grip for a second. It was just long enough for me to run to the door, release the lock and race down the hall!

I pushed the elevator button. It was slow responding so I took the stairs. I was relieved when the cold air hit my face at the exit. Walking along the garden path, lovely even in winter, my racing heart began to slow. I began to feel chilled in the wintery air, having left my coat behind. I had been an idiot, no question about it. I could have played things cooler, had a good meal and still kept my clothes on. The man was a creep, but I didn't need to rub it in his face! He would surely fire me. Now ComCen was a thing of the past and good jobs were scarce. I was an idiot!

I was about 3km from home, but I knew the way, so I decided to walk. It would do me good. I had always been a hot head. I was prone to speaking first, thinking later. Rick never acted that way. He kept his cool and probably Nash was right, Rick and Andy were probably eating coconuts in the jungle. I have to think that way. The power of positive thinking; that's what I needed. I had tried the power of negative thinking and see what it got me! I had been walking quite fast and Barb's little house was coming up. Barb and I have the same day off so she was likely to be home. I needed her shoulder to cry on, but I was almost ashamed to confess the tantrum I had had. It was kid stuff, I should have known better.

The dogs were barking before I entered the front gate. Open popped the door and when she spread her arms, I just fell in! How wonderful to have a friend like Barb. By the time I got the whole story out, my best dress was well soaked with tears, and Barb's was pretty damp as well. "Mattie," she said, "God how I wish I had been there. You were magnificent! You went out in a blaze of glory! I am so proud of you, girl! You gave that tomcat what he deserved. This calls for a major celebration. Let's go out to dinner, my treat."

Barb always could turn something bad into something good. We walked to our favorite little bar and ordered steaks and beer. What a day!

9/15/42 When I entered the ComCen Personnel Department to turn in my badge and collect my final paycheck, I was greeted by the assistant manager, Mary Smythe. I barely knew the woman. I had to be "debriefed" she said and asked me to follow her into her office. Then, instead of sitting behind her desk, she took a chair close to mine. I must have had a puzzled look on my face, because she whispered, "We all know what you did yesterday. Nash's driver keeps us informed. A bunch of us want to invite you as guest of honor to a little bash tonight after work. We have all been victims of that pervert, but none of us had the guts to tell him off. But you did and we love you for it!" With that she leaned over and gave me a peck on the cheek. I was flabbergasted! Instead of a screw up I was a hero! I had struck a blow for womankind!

"I would love to come," I said. I couldn't say more. The words were stuck in my throat. I went right home and washed and pressed that best dress again. It was Barb who came by at six, (she was in on it too), and for the second day in a row I had a rollicking good time with women who had "been there"!

9/16/42 It is time to take stock. My status with the US Army is unclear. Rick is MIA, missing in action, neither dead nor alive. I get "subsistence" from the army and I can do a lot more babysitting, so I will get by financially I think. I get lonely so Barb's invitation sounds very tempting, except for her dogs. Better to take life day-by-day, not commit myself.

9/21/42 Sat for Nancy Nash's kids today. When she paid me she gave my hand a squeeze and looked me straight in the eye with a kind of sad tired expression. She seemed ready to say something, then changed her mind. She knew!

9/27/42 I think what I really need is another steady job. I don't really have a babysitting mentality. Squealing kids tend to drive me a little crazy. Grownups are bad enough, some anyway. I miss Rick. Rick kept me on an even keel. He was calm and cool, and to fess up, that sometimes got me mad too. I am probably a royal pain to live with, except that I am cute, or so Rick says. I start job-hunting tomorrow.

9/30/42 Barb tells me that the Coast Guard is looking for civilian women volunteers to assist on patrol boats, but not listing it in the paper. Applicants must be Australian citizens and be physically fit with good eyesight. Cruise duration will average two months, but will not exceed three months. She tells me to get off my butt and apply. Darn it, I think I will!

10/16/42 I have just completed an intense two-week training course for life on an Australian Coast Guard cutter as a Civilian Assistant. I have the lowest rank of anyone on the cutter, but hey, I'm on board! I am from now on forbidden to keep this personal record, so as I lock up the house, I am leaving it in my dresser drawer. Goodbye, dear diary.

CHAPTER FIVE
JOE'S RECORD

Day 74. We had returned to the compound, four men carrying the litter with a very impatient "G" on board. It appeared that nothing had been disturbed or stolen. It was also clear, by observing boot prints left by the soldiers, that they took the trail south. The coastal town of Lae was in that general direction, according to Kato. It was from there that Kato had gone AWOL. Kato seemed to fear recapture, although I doubted that the Japanese would be still looking for him. I had barely slept the night before, so I retired to our hut early in the afternoon. Kato was already there, sound asleep. I was stretched out on my bed, starting to drift off when I felt Kan shaking me awake. I was rather annoyed. Was it another dogfight in the air? There had been several recently between Japanese Zeros, (according to Kato) and sleek US fighter planes with a twin fuselage which Kato could not identify. It was exciting to watch, but not then; my body craved sleep.

Again I was shaken! Kan was bending over me, our faces almost touching. His eyes were wild with excitement, but I could not comprehend what he was trying to tell me. Then sensing another presence, I looked beyond his face and was startled to see three natives with painted faces standing at the foot of my bed. I had visitors! I sat up instantly! Fortunately Kato awoke at the same time and immediately stepped forward to greet them. He had met these men before. Now, introducing me, he explained that they were Peace Trekkers. A practice introduced originally by missionaries, these trekkers walked the length of the island, visiting each tribe along the way. It was their mission to bring more friendship and understanding between tribes. They were familiar with the many tribal languages and could converse well enough to be bearers of the news. Their arrival was a major social event. Sleep would need to wait.

When I reached the ground I saw that they had a donkey, tied by the long house, and a small nanny goat. The goat was huddled up to the donkey, as if for protection from the swarm of children crowed about them. Kan said that the donkey was to carry things and the goat was for milk. The donkey's pack had been unloaded and sat in the long- house. Our chickens walked about the yard as usual, quite unimpressed by the visitors.

A party was held that afternoon in the long-house with "G" sitting much like a king on his throne. It was show time for the trekkers, dancing to the drums and shouts of the men. Next came food and drink, served by the women. Finally, as dusk was approaching, came the event they were all waiting for, the telling of stories. The trekkers went first, speaking and acting out the events in the news.

The first thing the trekkers described was their close encounter with the Japanese squad of soldiers that had terrified us. The trekkers were walking north and they had heard the squad coming down the trail long before their arrival, because their boots made so much noise on the path. The bare footed trekkers had ample time to hide in the jungle, their only concern being, keeping the animals quiet! Unfortunately, the donkey did pray several times, but this only seemed to frighten the soldiers and make them move faster! This was so funny, especially the way the trekkers acted it out, that "G" and the whole audience was roaring with laughter. It felt good to have something to laugh about. "G" followed with what was clearly the story of his brush with the Japanese – and so it went, story after story, late into the night.

The following day was rainy, good for sleeping. There was little activity in the compound, but that evening the party continued as before. From the stories, we learned that the Japanese occupied most of the seacoast towns and settlements on the eastern shore. Milne Bay at the southern tip of Papua was an exception. This was the location of an Australian base and airfield. The trekkers had been there only a few weeks before and were presently trekking north. One tribe to the south attempted to ambush a platoon of Japanese soldiers, but the natives were all machine-gunned to death. The message from this was clear: Arrows were not able to fight guns so natives must appear to be neutral in order to survive! All-in-all, the stories we heard from the trekkers were very depressing. The enemy juggernaut seemed invincible!

Kato, on the other hand, saw in the report our means of escape. If we moved quickly, he reasoned, we might reach Milne Bay and join the Allied forces in the fighting. I pointed out that the enemy was well entrenched in Lae and Buna, areas we would need to pass through. I also pointed out that he, Kato, looked very Japanese and would certainly be captured or killed. He countered that if we remained here the

Japanese would sooner or later reach us and we would suffer the same fate. He seemed to have a point.

The next morning the trekkers were preparing to leave when Kato and I sat down with them to get their advice regarding Kato's idea. They knew our story and recognized the dangers we both faced. They debated the idea among themselves and with us. (Fortunately Kan was there too to interpret.) After almost an hour, a new and better plan had been hatched – instead of continuing north as planned, the trekkers would return south with us since they knew the dangerous sections and alternate routes around them. Kato, since his face would give him away, would be painted as a Peace Trekker, hiding his features. I, on the other hand, would be too hard to disguise. I would continue to be the tall Aussie civilian with no memory.

Suddenly, Kan, realized that he might lose us, burst from our group and raced to see "G." It was only then that I discovered that Kan was an orphan and that "G" was his caregiver. Poor Kan was pleading for permission to go with us, tears streaming down his face, "G" holding him to his massive chest. The two talked quietly for some time as we stood back at a respectful distance. Finally a decision was made: Kan would become an apprentice Peace Trekker and go with us. Trekking would give him a fine education about the world beyond and he would still visit home several times a year.

The general plan in trekking was to be, as often as possible, an overnight guest in a tribal village. When this was not possible they would camp along the trail. For the three trekkers this meant taking turns between sleeping under an animal hide and sitting guard while tending the campfire. There seemed to be some question, in the mind of the trekkers, as to Kato's and my ability to stand such rigors. "G" assured them however, with much laughter and pointing with his finger that we were tougher than we looked. That was the final blessing we needed!

The next two days were spent in preparation. The trekkers painted Kato and Kan in brilliant colors and taught the various dances to be used at festivities. Kan kept running to the water tub to see his reflection! Kato was given extra speech training so that he would sound less like a Harvard medical student and more like a native trekker.

Day 79. The donkey was loaded with three additional animal hides, a cook pot, and a water bag. She seemed to require a bit of tugging with a lead rope to get her started, but the goat required no rope since she walked close by her big friend wherever she went. It was a beautiful relationship.

We traveled light. Each had a pouch of dried food and a water bag. Each of the tribesmen carried a bow and quiver of arrows; I was given a machete in a leather scabbard. I still had the floppy Aussie hat that stayed with me as I fell from the sky and my old leather flight jacket. It would keep me warm and dry in the rain. I was ready!

This was a day for bidding "G" and all the other members of his tribe a fond farewell. These gracious, simple people had saved the lives of both Kato and me, nurtured us to good health, and now, even allowed us to take away Kan, their young "Prince and Heir Apparent." We had a lot to be grateful for.

CHAPTER SIX
RECOLLECTIONS BY ANDY

May 6, 1943 The moment I stepped out of the plane at Melbourne Airport I was surrounded by friends asking where I'd been. I gave the old lips-are-sealed sign and checked in with my company CO, Captain Marks. He indicated that he was glad I was still alive and noted that I'd lost weight. Then he rang up ComCen and told me that Nash was waiting to see me. I got a jeep ride to ComCen. General Nash, I felt sure, would take immediate steps to secure Rick's rescue. Nash was one to take care of his own. As I entered through the security gate at ComCen I could feel a pleasant change from the frantic mood of a year before; the war was turning around.

As I passed by the glass doors of the "Switchboard Room," I peeked in hoping to get a glimpse of Mattie. She was not there; perhaps she had a different shift. Arriving at Nash's office, his secretary said, "Good morning Corporal Andrews. Go right in." I gave him the old, "Corporal Andrews reporting, Sir!" and he put me at ease.

"You're a corporal?" he said, "Well I'll have to do something about that. Sit down Corporal and give me the whole bloody story. What the hell went wrong up there? Here, have a cigar." Being a non-smoker now, I respectfully declined the cigar, but gave him a detailed account of our unsuccessful mission to Mount Wilhelm. We must have talked for fully an hour.

He seemed to take it all in, but several of his comments surprised me. When I described Rick's decision to follow the Ramu River, which I thought was brilliant, Nash retorted, "Damned idiot! You don't fool the enemy by letting yourself be seen! I should've picked a man with more brains. He's not one of us you know, he's an American on detached service." Then he went on, "Don't worry about Billings getting out. The north coast is secure now. All he needs to do is walk out, that is if the Fuzzys don't get hungry and eat him – ha, ha, ha."

I was so mad I could spit, but of course I didn't. I tried to change the subject, mentioning that I would be looking up Mrs. Billings. The general frowned and said, "A word of caution Corporal. My advice is to steer a wide path around that woman. I had to let her go some time ago. Couldn't have a woman with her reputation in ComCen. She is a whore. You've heard the expression: 'When the cat's away the mouse will play.' Captain Billings deserves better!"

I stood up, saluted and said, "Permission to leave, Sir" It was granted and I left in a daze, repeating over and over the words he had said. Could it be true? I did not know Mattie well enough to be sure. I had only met her that one time. She seemed nice enough. One thing was for sure, I didn't like Nash's sense of humor and I felt disillusioned about his attitude toward Rick.

There was a bus stop across from ComCen, with a bench under a tree. I sat and thought about my next move, letting a couple of busses pass me by. Finally it became clear: no matter what Mattie was guilty of, I had to see her. The next bus took me to the corner of her street. It was a neat little white house with a rear deck. The lawn was nicely mowed, but there were no flowers in the garden. It was a crisp fall day in May, but no smoke rose from the chimney. I knocked on the door. Knocked again, louder. Then I saw the note thumb-tacked by the letter slot. "Deliver all mail to # 37 until otherwise notified." I had just past #37 a few doors back; it was where the dogs barked. I returned and knocked at #37. The noise was enough to split your eardrums, but when the door opened the barking stopped. Standing before me was a nice looking woman in her thirties, a bit disheveled maybe, but nice to look at. She said, "Hello soldier, what can I do for you?" like she really meant it.

"I'm Andrews," I said. "I was hoping to see Mrs. Billings. Is she away?"

"Well I'll be damned! You're Andy! Come in. The dogs wont hurt you. They may lap you to death, but you'll enjoy it. Have a seat. Tea or coffee?"

After coffee and scones we got down to serious conversation. Her name was Barb and she and Mattie were like that (she crossed her fingers). She had a husband somewhere up north and she missed him terribly. Mattie was serving her country on a Coast Guard patrol boat. Her tours were about two and a half months long, more or less. She might be back any day now. Then she had a month of time off during which they would "raise a little hell" together. I gave a somewhat sanitized version of what I had gone through and my suspicions about Rick's fate. When I mentioned that I had been to see Nash and his comment about Rick (I left out the part about Mattie) she just said, "That creep!"

I wanted to hear her version of why Mattie got fired, but did not dare ask. Barb explained that she had the evening shift at ComCen, and had to leave soon. This was my cue to leave. She said if I wanted to talk further to just stop by. She said she would let me know when Mattie was home, so I gave her my phone number, thanked her and left. I took the bus to the base and when I walked into the orderly room, Captain Marks handed me four sets of sergeant stripes, staff sergeant stripes no less! "General Nash's orders." he said, "Are you pimping for the general, Andrews? He must like you!" I just took the stripes and smiled. I picked up bedding at the supply shed and hit the line at the mess tent. It was nice to be home again.

About a week later, the CQ gave me a phone number to call. It was Barb. Mattie was back and sufficiently rested to enjoy a dinner party and she was dying to meet me. Was I free next Saturday evening at six? I told her I'd be there and began sewing my new stripes on my dress uniform. Come Saturday evening I went to the motor pool and asked for a jeep, expecting to have to beg for it, but with my new stripes on my arm, I got waved though the gate! Rank has privilege.

Well Barb and Mattie had cooked the meal together at Mattie's house. Seems Mattie found Barbs dogs a bit much too. They had splurged and bought flowers for the table. I put the beer and wine I'd brought in the fridge. It was shaping up to be a lovely evening.

I had expected to see Mattie in uniform, but she explained that she was a civilian now for a whole month and could wear what she damn well pleased! Barb had relayed my Papua story, of course, but Mattie wanted to hear it from me too. I described what I had seen of the native village where I suspected Rick might be and tried to assure her that the natives were friendly. I had reached the time when I should have mentioned my visit with Nash, but decided to skip it.

Then Barb pipes up, "Andy, you forgot the best part. Tell her what Nash said when you saw him." So I repeated what I had told Barb before, adding that I disliked his humor.

Then Mattie said that there was much more than that to dislike about General Nash. Then she proceeded to tell me in detail about how and why she had been fired. When I then revealed Nash's defamatory statements about her, Mattie turned several shades of purple and just sat there shaking her head, and letting the tears flow. I had called a spade a spade, and now I was regretting it. Barb was hugging Mattie by now and thanking me profusely for blurting out the whole truth. I had said the right thing after all. I had revealed Nash's true miserable character. It hit me then that the staff sergeant stripes I was wearing was Nash's attempt to shut me up, make me his boy. Now all three of us had reason to hate the man. What a creep! Well, with this bond of emotion, of hatred, joining us, Barb got out her berry pie with ice cream on top and we polished off the entire thing! It was a good party after all.

CHAPTER SEVEN
JOE'S RECORD

We made good progress on the first day, day 80, despite the roughness of the path. Day 81 brought us along side an open meadow brilliant with yellow flowers. We stopped here for a while to rest, enjoying the view, but when Kan began to venture out among the blooms, the trekkers called him back explaining that snakes loved this place too. The lack of trees here gave us a chance to see the mountains rising steeply in the distance. One peak appeared especially tall, dominating the landscape. We were about to move on when we spotted a column of black smoke rising from the jungle on the other side of the bog, perhaps ten kilometers away. The trekkers told us, through Kan, that this was an evil sign and we must move on immediately!

I could see that the further we walked, the more nervous Kato became. This was the path that Kato had traveled in his race to flee the Japanese, so he was able now to point out places where he had hidden. Twice now we have met other tribal men on the trail. It was always an occasion to stop and ask if they had encountered the Japanese, or had any other news that the trekkers could use. One man who looked quite tired and worn was offered a drink of milk from the goat. To my surprise, the man simply bent down and squirted a few mouthfuls directly into his mouth, never spilling a drop! Then, smiling and rubbing the goat behind her ears, he thanked the trekkers and walked on. This was a man who knew goats!

About mid-afternoon we came to a juncture in the path and were told by the trekkers that we would meet another tribe now and would stay the night. The trekkers reminded Kan that he must behave, do the dances properly, and not ask for more food than was offered. The path led us east toward the river. As we entered their village we were greeted first by a group children, wildly screaming, obviously thrilled at seeing the trekkers with their painted faces. Then the chief appeared, looking very worried and puzzled. He was not expecting to see the trekkers again so soon. Why were we traveling south instead of north? Had we been turned back by the Japanese?

Just how the trekkers responded to all their questions, I do not know, but we were treated like visiting royalty. There was dancing and feasting late into the night. As an "Aussie man" I was not expected to dance, but I must say, Kato and Kan performed well indeed! The best part, however, was the refreshing bath in the river and the soft grass mattress I eventually tumbled onto.

At daybreak, we got a fine breakfast and advice from the chief before departing. Japanese scouting parties had been spotted. He suggested that I act very old, walk with a staff and support myself on Kan, and let Kan carry the machete. If I looked really old and feeble they might not shoot me. I was all for that, so my image changed immediately. My beard and hair were long by then so, to "age" me, the Trekkers painted it dirty white. They all agreed that I looked very old and feeble, not worth shooting. So with much cheering from the children and a wave from the chief, we left those friendly people and resumed the trail south.

Kan clearly loved his status as my protector and walking companion. Kan and I walked side-by-side with my hand on his shoulder, just as the chief advised. I found that the bamboo staff that I carried in my other hand seemed to improve my walking. One of the Trekkers walked well in advance of the rest of us, as a scout to give warning if needed. The other two trekkers, leading the donkey and goat, come next, while Kan and I took up the rear.

As the days went by, we met with several more tribes. They were always friendly and welcoming and a fine source of information about what the Japanese were up to. Kan could usually understand the drift of their dialects and took great pride in being my interpreter. Kan, always so eager to learn new words, now speaks fairly understandable English. Walking side-by-side, we are able to talk as we walk. His parents, he told me, had both died from a fever before he was old enough to remember them. He described growing up with his new father, "G," and how he was always given special privileges because he would some day be the chief. He was quite matter-of-fact about it! I felt that was a shocking way to raise a child, but I kept it to myself. (I find the concept of royal privilege somewhat revolting.) For my part, I taught him things I knew about the world, about the pyramids in Egypt, for example. Talking helped make the miles slip by more easily.

The trail was better in this region and I estimated that we averaged twenty to thirty kilometers a day. We had been trekking for over a week now in a southeasterly direction, following the river valley. Kato called it the Ramu River. Most of the tribal villages we visit are along the shoreline. On our right, the mountains rise up like the back of a huge dinosaur, often shrouded in clouds. I was told that they were the Owen Stanley Mountains and they looked formidable!

Day 95. The trail was now headed toward the south and was growing steeper. It was cold and misty, but the trekkers, despite their lack of clothing, seemed unperturbed. So far we had not seen the Japanese although the tribal elders had. They told of soldiers arriving on motorcycles, always several in a group. The meetings seemed to be good will gestures by the Japanese to ensure tribal neutrality. I was sure both sides were fearful of the other. The tribal history of head hunting gave the enemy reason to think twice. The port town of Lae, Kato told me, was off to our left by about eighty kilometers. The Japanese had a large encampment there and Kato's fear was palpable. Warplanes were in the sky and these frightened the natives most of all.

Day 97. The inland town of Wau lay directly on our path. There was no way to avoid it. On their previous trek, coming north, the Peace Trekkers had met a number of Australian civilians on the track to Milne Bay, escaping the inevitable invasion of Wau. Milne Bay, five hundred kilometers away at the southern tip of Papua, was home to an Australian naval base. An alternative escape route was the fearsome Kokoda track over the Owen Stanley Mountains to Port Moresby, the capital city of Papua. It was shorter by far, but very challenging to walk according to the trekkers.

The town of Wau, Kato told me, grew initially when Australian miners discovered gold and established a small mine. The mine had since been abandoned, but the town remained. The night before we were to enter Wau, we all sat down to confer and weigh the risks. First we had to get through Wau alive; the Kokoda decision could come later. The town had been quiet on the trekker's last visit; perhaps it still was.

The final plan: In the morning, one of the trekkers would remove his body paint, so as not to look unusual, and scout out the town. We would wait until he returned for us. None of us had a better plan so, in the morning, off he went. When he returned about an hour later he was smiling broadly – the town was deserted. So, after our scout got a bright new paint job, we all set out again.

It was a bleak looking town, with a down-on-it's-luck appearance common to mining towns. There were several bars and a dry goods store that appeared to have been closed for years. There was an airstrip with no planes. Then to our surprise we saw a general store with an old man sitting in a rocking chair on the porch! He waved us over. He spoke first, "Howdy mates! Welcome to Wau. Didn't I catch sight of you boys going the other way bout a month ago? Can't cha make up yer mind? He, he, he!"

This time it was my turn to do the talking. I said, "I am aiming to get to Australia and my Peace Trekker friends are trying to help me. Got any advice?"

"Hell yes," he thundered, "Don't follow them other idiots to Milne. They's walking into a trap. Them yellow bastards will capture Milne next, you mark my words! Hell it's safer here. Nothing here worth fighting for. If you want to get back home take the Kokoda track. Japs wont be going that way, they ain't that dumb, mark my words. If they go after Port Moresby it'll be by sea, not by the Kokoda track, mark my words!" It struck me that the old man knew what he was talking about and I for one did "mark his words." I still had a few pound notes in my money belt and was able to treat my friends to some of the old man's Australian candy bars and his last bottles of warm beer. "No telling when the plane will come back with more," he said.

It was tempting to just remain there with this colorful old sage, but we had to move on, and quickly. By taking the Kokoda Track, it seemed, we would find safety more quickly, and more certainly, than by taking the long route to Milne Bay. The others voiced their agreement and thus the die was cast. The trekkers said that by pushing ourselves, we could reach Kokoda in six days, but this meant more nights on the trail, no resting in the hospitality of friendly tribes. It was agreed, so off we went.

Again the trail followed a river valley, much narrower than the Ramu and the mountains to our right were even closer and more ominous. Kan and I trudged side-by-side, my hand lightly touching his young shoulder. My shoes had begun to come apart and my socks were in shreds and I could tell that Kan was concerned for my comfort. This dear boy who walked barefoot in the rain and over sharp rocks, he was concerned for me. From the day I had come down from the tree, he had watched over me. He clearly revered me, and what had I done in return? I had tempted him to leave the safety of his home to follow me into dangers, dangers that might easily cost him his life. How unfair, how selfish I had been! I loved Kan dearly and the thought of him being in danger terrified me.

Kan seemed to be reading my thoughts, because he looked up and said, "We OK Joe. We OK!" and gave me a reassuring smile. Yes – we would be OK.

CHAPTER EIGHT
MATTIE'S DIARY

5/16/43 Last evening Barb had my welcome home dinner party and it was one for the record books. Corporal Andrews was there, except he is now Staff Sergeant Andrews. Andy explained how their plane went down and how they were separated. He thinks Rick is waiting out the war with a tribe of natives. He described their village, how neat and clean it was, and the probable reason why the village was deserted. Crazy trigger-happy Japs! On the other hand, if the natives had not been scared out of their village, the Japs might have walked in and murdered them all! He also told us how they found the plane and the gruesome death that helped him give up smoking. Hey, whatever it takes!

Andy, bless his heart, saved the best part for last. He told me word for word what that devil Nash is telling people about me. It is not fit to print even in your pages, dear diary! I hope I get the change to fix his wagon some day! Maybe God will nail him with a bolt of lightening! What a creep!

After Andy returned to the base, Barb and I sat up really late and she decided to spend the night. If she had gone home her dogs would have awakened all the neighbors. We talked about our husbands and what they might be doing. Her husband, Pat, has been stationed in Port Moresby on the lower west coast of Papua for over a year. Last year he was in a terrible battle with the Japanese on the Kokoda track. Thank God he wasn't hurt! God, I hate this war!

5/17/43 Slept late. Barb has the evening shift, (even on Sunday, of course). I spent the day cleaning house. I have a whole month to do something, but I have not made up my mind what it should be. I will go up to see Mum and Dad in Sydney next week. That tends to be depressing. They dwell on the gloomy side of everything. But I love them, deed I do.

5/24/43 I am back home. Mum is knitting mittens for soldiers and Dad is an air raid warden. They were glad to see me and in better spirits than what I expected. A whole week with them is enough, however, and it is sad that I feel that way, but I do.

5/27/43 Poor Barb got a letter from the Australian Army yesterday with both good news and bad. Pat is on his way home to be discharged, but he had been seriously wounded in the combat on the Kokoda track. He had lost both legs and had been recuperating in the hospital in Port Moresby for much of the past year, too sick to be transported, but never telling Barb in his letters that he was injured! All he had said was that he was unable to get leave. Now, well enough to be released, he was coming to the veteran's hospital in Melbourne.

I had never met Pat, but now Barb and I would see him in a few days. Barb was in a state of shock. She was hugely relieved that Pat was alive, but terribly hurt that she had been deceived, despite Pat's admirable reasons for doing so. Then I thought of Rick. If Rick were gravely injured, would I want to know, or is the happy fiction of Rick sitting comfortably by a native campfire better? It is a hard call, but I think I would prefer the truth. In the meantime, Barb sobbed her heart out on my shoulder and I was glad to be there for her. God, I hate this war!

6/2/43 Today's the day. I drove because Barb is acting very unreliable. Visiting hours begin at 10AM and we were on time. I sat in the lounge reading magazines while Barb went in. Actually I did not read a thing, just stared at pages, seeing only Rick and wondering how he might look now. His beard would be huge and his hair long, but those incredible mischievous eyes would sparkle out to me, invite me in. Every day I think, maybe today he will burst through the door and take me in his arms – god what arms!

I was off in this fantasyland when Barb touched my shoulder. She wanted to introduce me to Pat so I followed her in. His cheerful smile was what hit me first. No pain registered on his face, just joy and friendship. He was clean-shaven and was sitting propped up with a medal pinned to his pajamas. Barb said she had already given him hell for telling lies and a spanking would come later. For me, he repeated that, "He couldn't wait for that spanking." After about half an hour of cheerful banter, a nurse called a halt, saying Pat needed a bit of rest and we were ushered out. As we left the building Barb thanked me again for going along and said, "I was afraid it might be worse. He is the same old Pat, almost. We'll make a life."

I had seen a sign at the hospital door, "Nurses/aides/help of all kind needed. Apply at desk." That night I thought about volunteering during my month off of Coast Guard duty. Seeing all the wounded all day – that would be depressing. But suppose Rick were to arrive in the hospital, wounded, and I were there to greet him, care for him! Tomorrow I will sign up.

6/3/43 The hospital is about three kilometers away, an easy bike ride, and the air was chill and crisp. Barb was emotionally calm now and could drive herself. They put me to work immediately in the kitchen washing pots and pans, BIG pots and pans! Big enough to cook a small person in! My supervisor, a large colored woman, pointed out a few spots I had missed, and said, "You'll get the hang of it, honey, just like I did." And so I did, but it was a hard day. As I peddled home in the half-light of evening, I felt very good about myself. Tomorrow I would do an even better job.

6/10/43 See that date. I've been neglecting my diary. After a week in the kitchen I was put on "Paper Boy" duty and given a map of the rooms and hallways. I push a little cart with records and urine samples and whatever, from hither to yon and back. Thank god for the map. I still get mixed up sometimes, and I'm never as fast as they want me to be, but it is better than pots and pans. I have seen Pat, briefly, and he is now wheeling himself in a chair, or with Barb pushing. Those are good signs.

Some of the patients are Papuan natives, "Fuzzy Wuzzys" according to Pat. The hospital in Port Moresby was overwhelmed so the long-term cases were being sent here. These brave men assisted the Aussies by carrying out the wounded on the Kokoda Track, and often becoming casualties themselves. Just to walk the track was a terrible experience, Pat told me, but to fight there was nightmarish!

Once I was able to take my lunch break with Barb and Pat in the sunroom. When the subject shifted to the natives, Pat confided with tears in his eyes, that it was two Fuzzy Wuzzys that had saved his life, carrying him for two days on a crude stretcher in freezing conditions. "I would've died there on the damned track, but for them, and I was too damned sick to ask their names or even thank them!" he said, looking at the floor. Barb held his hand and I, for a change, said nothing. Then Barb had a great idea. "Let's go thank some of the Fuzzy Wuzzys now," she said and off they went down the hall!

6/16/43 Pat was released from the hospital, but must check back once a week. Fitting the wheelchair in Barb's car was a challenge better suited to Houdini, but we did it. And the dogs, well they damn near licked him to death!

6/25/43 I am back in my freshly pressed Coast Guard uniform and reporting for duty at 1300 hours. Barb, Pat, Andy and I had a nice party last night, all in honor of ME! Pat was in a great story telling mood replaying some of the pleasanter things that went on in Port Moresby before the Kokoda battle began. The Fuzzy Wuzzys loved to dance and often put on shows that were much more interesting than the ancient movie reruns in the army theater. One show, just before the Kokoda conflict began, was put on by a group that called themselves "Peace Trekkers," brightly painted dancers whose mission was to bring news, and spread peace and understanding between tribes. They had just come across the Kokoda Track with the Japs close on their heels! The news they brought that day was bad indeed!

So, bye-bye dear diary. I'll be gone for another two or three months. You should be nice and warm in my dresser drawer.

CHAPTER NINE
JOE'S RECORD

Day 102 We arrived at Kokoda. Kokoda was located on a high plateau. There was an airstrip, but again, no aircraft. This was an Australian outpost and a small cadre of soldiers was there to greet us. The tension in the air was electric. The old storekeeper had been wrong about what the Japanese would do, but it was too late for us to change our plan. We were committed! To reach the trail to Milne Bay now would mean walking into enemy hands. The Japanese were coming in huge numbers and would surely overwhelm their meager force, but they intended to slow their progress as much as possible. Port Moresby itself was short of troops and supplies; time was of the essence!

We made our way immediately to the commanding officer, a weather-beaten colonel with sad eyes and a welcoming smile. I explained what I knew about myself and how I'd gotten there, which wasn't much. His advice was quick and to the point: Go to the supply shed for warmer clothes, boots, mosquito nets and ponchos, especially for the nearly naked trekkers, and hit the Kokoda Track running! When I mentioned that the Peace Trekkers had never been on the Kokoda Track, he gave us a man, a Private Nugent, to go with us to keep us from getting lost. I thanked him, saluted and left.

Private Nugent was a godsend. Barely older than a boy, and only a little taller than Kan, he knew the track well and possessed the energy of youth. He had an Enfield rifle slung over his shoulder and handed one to me as well. He said a quick farewell to his friends, realizing, I am sure, that he might soon be the only one alive. As we began our trek, Nugent explained that although the track was only about 70 kilometers as the crow flies, the actual distance was a great deal longer, approximately 96 kilometers. He warned us that we would climb to over 7000 feet at one point, where it would be extremely cold, then climb down into steamy mosquito-infested jungle! It would test us to the limit, he said. (He also advised me of the actual calendar date: My "day 102" was really July 3, 1942, so I shall indicate the date properly hereafter.) After that exchange we stopped talking and applied all our energy to walking.

We had not gone far when the rain began and we were glad of the ponchos and extra clothing. The rain, coupled with the high elevation and wind, soon tempered my initial optimism; it would be a hard slog!

7/12/42 Nine days of terrible trekking, mostly walking single file in the rain, have passed since my last entry. It was everything Private Nugent had warned us of, and more. Without Nugent to guide us, the donkey to carry the gear, the goat to nourish our bodies, and the enduring strength of the trekkers, we would surely have been lost and died out there!

Today we entered the village of Ower's Corner that marks the western end of the track. We still had a day's walk to reach the city of Port Moresby, but now it was easy – a paved road.

I believe the Peace Trekkers came through the best. Both Kato and Private Nugent, however, appear to be suffering from dengue fever (Kato's diagnosis) and I am so tired I am sleepwalking! I suspect the enemy is close behind us, though we have not seen them – but now Aussie soldiers are everywhere! Then, surprise! An Aussie army truck pulled up and we were all (even including the animals) given a ride into the city and to the Australian Army Headquarters. We reported in, of course, Nugent describing the dire conditions at the Kokoda outpost. Then we were all transported to the army hospital for a check-up and a bit of R&R. What bliss!

7/13/42 Ah, but the bliss was short lived. Both Kato and Private Nugent did have dengue as Kato thought. They were both admitted to the hospital immediately, but seeing that Kato was Japanese, the staff felt compelled to have an armed guard beside his bed. When I explained that Kato Matsuri was a US citizen, Harvard medical student and loyal American, they just looked at me and laughed. They were labeling all Japanese as the enemy – that angered me!

Kan and the Peace Trekkers were given a physical check-up too, after I insisted on it. They were OK and were moved, along with the animals, in with a native tribe near the city. As for me, they looked upon me as a very special case: I was not exactly crazy, but I wasn't sane either. A doctor in the mental ward, Dr. Moe Smith, was to study me and make a decision about where I belonged. In the meantime I was allowed to roam the halls and sit in the patient lounge.

7/14/42 The patients in the mental ward called Major/ Doctor Moe Smith, "Mad Moe" behind his back. After my first extended session with him, I felt the name was somewhat appropriate. He began with basics, like counting the number of fingers he held up. He tapped my head with his fingers and asked if it hurt. I gave him my life history as far as I knew it. He quizzed me on many topics. He was impressed by how much I knew of world geography and how little I knew of the war, beyond that told me by Kato. He checked my skill in writing and math. When I began a description of the chemical periodic table, he held up his hand. No question I was bright. Maybe I was a schoolteacher, or college professor. Could I recall that? He gave me a booklet of female names to read, searching out my wife. Nothing! "We will talk again soon." he said.

7/17/42 I was allowed to visit Private Nugent and spent some time with him, but Kato was off limits. I began to realize that Kato was in real danger for his life, not so much from Aussies, but from Japanese, if he were sent to a POW camp. I asked for and eventually got permission to see the hospital CO. I walked in, saluted and was put at ease. He was a bird colonel. He said, "This is odd. Your papers indicate you are Australian, but you salute like a Yank. Which are you?"

"I really don't know, Sir," I said and gave him a capsule report of my condition.

"You talk like a Yank too," he said. Then I went into my plea for Kato's safety and reasons for my concern. I told him that Kato had been a medical student at Harvard, and a US citizen, before being shanghaied into the Japanese forces. I even ventured to suggest that he might prove very useful in the hospital after the fighting intensified. He gave me a very penetrating look and said, "You've given this a lot of thought, I see. As soon as the doctors release him, I want both of you here so we can discuss this idea further. Write that man's name here for me. I never can remember Asian names. Thanks – whoever you are. You're dismissed."

7/19/42 I was working in the Clean Room, running the sterilizer, when an orderly tapped me on the shoulder and said to report to the CO, Colonel Farmer, on the double. The Clean Room supervisor gave me a "Boy-are-you-in-big-trouble" look and let me go. I arrived at the CO's office a bit out of breath, and was about to salute, when he said "Cut that crap! Sit down and have a shot of scotch with us. I have been saving this bottle for a special occasion. And before I forget, thanks for telling me about Kato."

There they sat, Kato and the colonel, side-by-side at a little table, like two old friends. I managed a "Thank you, Sir" and sat down with them on a chair he kicked in my direction.

"Kato has been telling me about his life at Harvard. One of his profs is an old friend of mine, from back when I studied in the States. Marty Goldenberg, the party man. When you get back, Kato, ask him if he remembers Ben Farmer, but be careful about calling him by the Party Marty nickname; he may have outgrown it."

We all sat quietly sipping scotch for a moment; then the colonel continued, "Here is the plan: I want Kato working here as a full doctor, starting now, and I want you, Joe, to be his assistant, constant companion, guardian really, to keep him alive. Trust nobody with a gun, or a hypodermic. I will address the staff, but some people are too angry at anything Japanese to listen. Then, God willing, if we all survive and a hospital ship one day sails for the States, I will bust my hump to see that you are both on board. Let's drink to that!"

We all rose to our feet, touched glasses and finished our drink. "Oh yes," he continued, "I almost forgot the matter of rank. Kato, you are now Doctor/Major Matsuri, United States Army, on detached service. After the smoke clears around here, I will call a man I know to make it official. Joe, now, you are a bit of a problem. You can't have a rank without a name, so you remain just plan "Joe," reporting to Kato. Any clown gives you trouble, send then to me. By the way, Joe, your friend Kato thinks you're a Yank too. Think about it. That's it, men, you're dismissed."

That evening at a staff meeting, the CO introduced us to the staff. He referred to Kato as a US Army major and doctor, here on detached service, and to me as his assistant. There followed many introductions and greetings, some sincere, but many that conveyed distrust. We were now part of the team, but we were very much on trial.

7/20 /42 This was our first day on the job. We had a lot to learn.

7/23/42 The Japanese assault on Port Moresby via the Kokoda Track had begun. A brief message came from the Kokoda defenders that morning, announcing the attack, before the line went dead. Private Nugent stopped by that morning to say goodbye. He had been released from the hospital and had joined the fighting here. He was a brave young man. (That was the last entry I made in my log until after the siege was over. There was no time for writing. The hospital chaplain made a poster that read, "God willing, our heroic force will prevail, and we will be among the living." Tragically, Private Nugent was killed on the Kokoda Track on August 16, 1942.)

9/30/42 Ten terrible weeks have passed. The rumor was right, the Japanese were beginning to retreat. Our work, however, was endless! We were all doing twenty-hour shifts, including the CO and his wife. On the good side: No one was still complaining about Kato's origins.

10/12/42 On the radio we received the tragic news that the USS Juneau was sunk near the fighting at Guadalcanal, killing all five brothers of the Sullivan family.

1/30/43 On this day some good news: The last Japanese have left Guadalcanal.

2/4/43 A hospital ship has sailed for the States, but Kato and I did not have the heart to leave the colonel. We did, however, polish off that bottle of scotch! The caseload had decreased a little. We now worked twelve-hour shifts.

3/1/43 On the radio: Eight Japanese troopships were sunk near New Guinea, causing heavy loss of life.

5/2/43 On this day some Japanese planes bombed Darwin, Australia, AGAIN! Why, I cannot imagine! What did they hope to accomplish? It appears that Japan had given up on taking New Guinea, but fighting still raged in the Solomon Islands.

6/27/43 Another hospital ship was in Port Moresby and this time Kato and I would be on board. We have made friends here, good friends, so parting was difficult. Kan, who had volunteered many long hours helping us at the hospital, was heartbroken. He wanted to come with us. Then the other Peace Trekkers came to my rescue, pointing out how he was needed to bring peace to those tribes that had suffered so much war. The thing that tipped the balance, however, was his desire to see "G" again, even if it meant re-crossing the Kokoda Track.

So with fresh clothes and hearty good wishes, Kato and I set out on the next stage of our adventure, to the United States of America.

CHAPTER TEN
RECOLLECTIONS BY ANDY

6/28/43 I had just gotten settled into the comfortable routine of camp life when Captain Marks walked into my private sanctum, the radio shop, and says, "Move yer lazy butt. Yer wanted back in Papua. What did you do up there, get some girl in trouble?"

"No such luck," I replied. "Why in hell must I return to that pest hole? Haven't I suffered enough?"

"Nash thinks you need another dose. Anyway, it's Port Moresby and their radio is shot to hell and Nash thinks only you can fix it. If you need helpers you find them there. Here's a list of the major damage. Take yer tools. Moresby's loaded with spare parts, but they need someone with a brain to stick them together. So pack up and kiss yer girls goodbye. Birdie will haul yer butt up there in the morning. Enjoy!"

Well, so much for the good life. Nothing can ruin your day like a visit from Marks. I called Pat and he gave me a few pointers about life in Moresby, the best bars (assuming they still exist), and friends to look up. I called Mattie, but she was working. I read the list Marks gave me and realized that I might be up there for months!

I called Birdie to find out how much gear I can bring and began weighing my stuff. I finished about mid-afternoon and headed out to get a good meal, perhaps my last for a long time!

6/29/43 Birdie and I were in the air by 0600 and had an uneventful flight to Moresby. It was dusk as we made our approach, the setting sun accentuating the damage of war. In the harbor the superstructures of sunken ships were standing silent guard, while among them moved a brightly marked hospital ship, smoke billowing from the stack. It was a sobering sight.

Birdie and I checked into HQ and got briefed. We were on time for supper in the mess, where Birdie got a warm reception. He flew this route often and always managed to have treats on board. This time it was a huge carton of candy. About then, the mess sergeant stepped up, counted the bars, eyeballed the group, and began cutting the bars in half. It made me appreciate the good life I'd just left back in Australia. Birdie would fly out in the morning with several of the recovering wounded that could travel. The look on their faces told it all. No child at Christmas ever looked happier; they were finally going home!

6/30/43 - 8/17/43 My first day started with a tour of the base, the hospital, and the city office compound. All had damage, some looked beyond repair. I was given two electricians, Jim and Tom. They had no radio know-how, but they would have to do. As it turned out, they were good at the grunt work: tearing out trash, installing new bread boards, and hauling supplies. Soon we had a working team, as they were installing as fast as I could design the circuits. For Tom, Port Moresby was home, and he knew just where to scrounge on the black market for equipment we needed. I was earning good pay, so in the evening, Tom would take us to out-of-the-way dives for good food and beer and I would foot the bill. That was good teamwork!

One day, when my crew had enough work to keep them busy, I looked for some clues that Rick might have been there. I was given hospital records to search, but no Billings was listed. When I was able to radio Milne Bay, I asked them to search. Again, nothing! I assumed the worst, but would never admit this to Mattie.

As first one radio network and then another came back into contact, our reputation grew. We were treated like heroes. Jim managed to parlay his fame into a relationship with one of the local beauties and began to come in late for work – very late. Then BOOM! Suddenly they were married and he was back on time again! I was glad I hadn't fired him.

I made schematics of all the networks, so the staff could make their own repairs in the future, and wrapped up my work there in Port Moresby. It had been a good experience for me and a chance to practice my fledgling engineering skills. I radioed Captain Marks and soon Birdie was there to haul me home.

CHAPTER ELEVEN
MATTIE'S DIARY

9/2/43 I am back home again and I am so tired I could sleep for a month! I cannot say what happened (Coast Guard rules) but it was horrible! It is amazing that I am alive and uninjured. I am going to bed and please, God, no dreams.

9/3/43 Barb took her day off to comfort me. She is my anchor. (No, that is too nautical. Barb is my rock.) After what happened I never want to see another ship, boat, cutter, anything that runs on water again! Barb understands. I have to forget. For that she is planning a wing-dinger of a party. She will have it here (the dogs, remember) and invite everyone, except General Nash. Barb's a real friend. So I will stop writing and fire up the sweeper. We must look good!

9/4/43 Saturday. The weather was raw and chilly, but it was party day, and my living room was full of Coast Guard men and ComCen women, my old buddies from the past. Andy showed up with a couple of his army friends. He was just back from some job in Port Moresby. No one there recalls seeing Rick, he says.

Barb and Pat were there of course. Pat looks great now, but was drinking too much. He was doing tricks on his wheelchair and flipped over backwards! (Thank God he wasn't hurt.) He calmed down after that and we moved his chair next to the fireplace because he feels the cold. That evening, Barb and Pat agreed to spend the night with me since the weather was really nasty outside. It was a fine party and my swan song to the Coast Guard. It is good to be home.

9/5/43 Sunday morning and it was still pouring rain outside. I was in the kitchen making coffee, hoping the aroma would wake up my sleepyhead friends, when in they burst. Their expressions said, "We know something you don't know!" and they were grinning ear to ear!

"Okay, out with it," I said. "Did you find out you're pregnant or something?"

"After breakfast." said Pat. "You have to feed us breakfast first. Boy! Am I hungry! What do you have?"

"Pat's right," chirps Barb. "Food first."

Well, it did no good to pry so I gave up, except I did offer a few suitable names for boys or girls, in case impending motherhood was the cause of their glee. Barb's expression seemed to tell me I was right. And Pat, damn it, he dawdled over his food and kept asking for more! I was taking dishes to the sink when he said, "Mattie, come over here and sit down." After I was seated, he said, "Mattie, when I was in the hospital in the Port Moresby, I was treated by a Japanese doctor who was a US Army major. He had an assistant named Joe who dressed my wounds and cared for all my needs. He was a wonderful man. Rumor had it that he was a patient himself, an amnesiac, one of Mad Moe's patients. Last night, Mattie, as I sat by your fireplace, I saw a picture of your Rick on the mantelpiece. Mattie, I am certain that Rick and Joe are the same man."

By this time I was sobbing so hard I am not sure who said what. Barb was holding me, keeping me from flying apart. Pat just sat there with the most beautiful smile on his face. The world was spinning. I ran and got the picture, one taken shortly after our wedding. Then I found more and showed them to Pat. He was still certain! I said, "Pat, you rascal, why didn't you tell me this last night?"

"What! And break up a beautiful party? I might never have gotten breakfast!" he said with a grin.

It was time for action. I called the CQ at Andy's unit and soon had Andy on the phone. I stammered out what Pat had said and his response was, "Great! Pack your bag. With an OK from Nash, we will be flying out Tuesday morning. Stay near a phone so I can call you back. Oh, and pack your pictures." It amazes me how men can be so cool, calm and collected. Guess that's why I'm a woman.

I spent the rest of the day packing and repacking. I wanted to wear a dress that Rick would recognize, one he loved. Rick had seldom expressed an opinion on my clothes, but it had to matter. I had to be prepared for having him not know me, perhaps learn to love me all over again. That night these thoughts pursued me all night. I didn't sleep a wink!

9/6/43 When Andy called back he said that General Nash was somewhat reluctant to authorize the flight, saying that "Joe" could return on the next patient transfer five weeks from now. Andy said, "He said this was a 'damn waste of petrol' but OK'd it anyway." What a lovable man.

9/7/43 A jeep picked me up at 7 AM and we were ready to take off by 7:30. It was just going to be two of us, however: the pilot, Sergeant "Birdie" Baker, and me. Andy could not go, which disappointed me, but I saw him briefly before we took off. He gave me a sisterly kiss and said, "Tell Rick I gave up tobacco. He hated the smell."

"We both did!" I replied.

It is hard to describe my emotions as we got closer and closer to Port Moresby. Birdie could see how shaky I was getting, swinging between desire to find my husband and fear of what I might find. He kept a running conversation going, pointing out interesting places along the route. I knew what he was doing and I tried to listen, but I don't remember a thing. I had made sandwiches for the flight, enough for three, so we had plenty to eat and that helped a little.

Birdie suggested that I take a nap on the bed in the back. I did, and the sound of the engine plus the lack of sleep the night before did the trick. When I woke up we were on the ground and it was dark as pitch. This was a war zone: no lights.

When I stirred, Birdie's voice came out of the darkness, "Thought you were going to sleep all night! I got a room for you in the hotel – better bed – let's go, it's 2 AM. We will check the hospital in the morning. I am pooped. Follow me."

9/8/43 As hotels go, it was a sad sight, but the bed was fresh and all that Birdie had said. I was asleep again in no time. This morning I found the bathroom at the end of the hall and discovered that the plumbing worked and even had warm water. So, wearing my red dress and with my face well scrubbed, I went down to the lobby to wait for Birdie. I expected him to come down the stairs from one of the rooms, but he walked in the front door instead. Seeing my puzzled expression, he explained that he always slept in the plane. "There is a big business in stolen aircraft here, especially on dark nights. Lose my plane and I'm in big trouble," he said. "We can get breakfast at the base mess, unless you want something fancier."

I told him that army food was fine, so off we went. It was a short walk and the early morning air felt delightful. We should not go to the hospital too early, he advised, and I knew he was right. He went on to say that we would see the commanding officer, Colonel Farmer, before we went looking for Rick. He acted as if he feared I might go racing about the hospital like an idiot! He must have heard about my reputation.

It was 0900 hours when we finally got cleared to see the colonel. The moment I met the man I liked him. Colonel Farmer had a fatherly manner, and when I showed him Rick's pictures, he leaped to his feet, ran to his door and asked his clerk to get Mad Moe on the double, and to bring his file on Joe. The colonel was as excited as I was. Moe, he explained, was the head doctor in the mental ward and was best acquainted with Joe's – Rick's – medical condition. There was no doubt, he said, that Joe and Rick were the same man. Then, almost as suddenly, the colonel sat down and with a pained expression on his face, said, "My God! I've sent your husband to the US thinking he was an American! He shipped out on the last hospital ship along with his Japanese-American friend. That was three months ago so he is there now. I'm so sorry, Mrs. – sorry, I didn't get your name."

"Matilda Billings, Sir, and you were correct, he is American. He is a US Army captain, although I did not know that until just before he left on that mission. He said I'd be safer not knowing, which galled me at the time. Thank God he is alive. I just knew he was alive somewhere. But how dreadful to lose one's mind. Did he really think his name was Joe?"

"He has amnesia, probably from trauma of some sort. Your husband has not lost his mind, Mrs. Billings, but he has lost a large portion of his memory. But memory can often be regained, especially with your help. Rick was confused about his nationality, but he struck me as an American. 'Joe' was just a name he pulled out of the air. Oh good, here's Moe," said the colonel.

Dr. Moe Smith had studied Rick for about a year, and he was a wealth of information if you talked "doctor-ese," but most of it went over my head. Rick's health had been restored after trekking the Kokoda Track, but despite his physical good health, his amnesia never improved. Moe described Rick as highly intelligent and went on to praise him for his help as an orderly during the dark days of the siege. I just sat there, glowing with pride, and letting the tears trickle down.

About then, Colonel Farmer raised his hand. "It's decision time," he said. "Mrs. Billings, have you been to the States? More to the point, do you have contacts there, and do you want to go? If you do, I will have my transportation clerk get you to the States as soon as possible."

My head was spinning. I had never been to the United States and I had never met Rick's parents in person, although we sent letters and photos all the time. "Oh yes," I stammered. "Rick promised to take me after the war to meet his family. We live in Melbourne now – did live. Sorry, I'm getting my words all tangled. Yes, yes, I want to go."

"Fine," he replied. "Do you need to return to Melbourne or can you leave from here? Work that out with Birdie and my clerk. When you get to the States, look up Major Kato Matsuri at Harvard University, where he was hoping to continue his medical studies. When you find Kato you may find Rick with him. My clerk will draw up the travel papers that you'll need.

Have a good trip! Now I have a dozen people waiting for me. You're dismissed!" When we stood, the colonel passed me a note with Kato Matsuri's name and probable address. I also got a big smile and a handshake. He was so nice. If the desk hadn't been in our way, I think I might have kissed him!

Outside the CO's office, Dr. Smith pointed the way to the clerk's office and wished me well. After the doctor had left, Birdie motioned me to a bench in the hallway. We sat down and Birdie said, "I've been doing some thinking about your trip to the States. I happen to know that General Nash hates your guts since you snubbed him one day. Andy may not have told you, but he had to really plead with the old buzzard to get you this trip to Moresby. Now if you show up back in Melbourne, I suspect he will kill your trip to the States, whether Colonel Farmer authorized it our not. Instead, let me drop you off in Sydney to visit your parents. From there you can hop the first ship to the States. I will report to Nash that Rick was not in Moresby after all, and that I dropped you off for some R&R with your parents in Sydney. It is true and it may keep Nash off your back. Think about it."

"I have, and I agree," I said. "But who told you about my Nash problems?"

Birdie replied, "Why, everyone on the base has heard about how you stiffed that old tomcat, and we are all damn proud of you. He had it coming and you had the guts to give it to him. You struck a blow for women everywhere!"

I was feeling a little breathless by this time. "Let's get that authorization," I said, and off we went.

CHAPTER TWELVE
JOE'S RECORD

6/28/43 Kato and I boarded the large white hospital ship, got our berth and were immediately put to work caring for patients. Colonel Farmer had included a stipulation in our travel papers that Kato and I continue to work as a team. I repeatedly had to reassure soldiers that Kato was not the enemy and, for some, this was a hard sell. I hoped, as at Moresby, the mood would change. For the present, we had a lot to learn. Most of our patients were bedridden and required constant attention, much of which was handled by women nurses. The smells were sickening and the ventilation was dismal, but I had no right to complain.

6/29/43 The ship got underway at dusk and as we began to move, the mood of our patients, as well as the ventilation, improved greatly. Some soldiers even started singing along with the band music coming over the speaker system. They were going home! For my part, I was not sure where I was going.

7/8/43 I have been too busy and too tired to write in this log. We made a stop at Guadalcanal and filled our ship to capacity. God, what horrors those men have suffered!

7/11/43 It was a Sunday and the chaplains were especially busy. The weather on deck was cold and damp, a pretty typical winter day in this latitude. The on-deck church service had been canceled. As compensation the mess provided the last of the fresh fruit that was loaded on board in Moresby. It was a telling sight to watch the wounded savoring the taste. It was easy to get caught up it the heartbreak of men who have lost so much and have so little to look forward to.

7/12/43 It was sunny and mild on deck and I was enjoying my break tucked behind a hatch, using it as a windbreak. Suddenly, to my surprise, one of the nurses rounded the corner and sat down beside me. "Hi Joe, I'm Kitty McNeil. Mind if I sit here, or was this spot reserved?"

"It was reserved for you," I ventured. I had observed Kitty ever since we left Moresby. What man could resist? She was very pretty and had an impish smile. She wore her little cap at a rakish angle, very un-military! "Beautiful day," I said.

"Hmmm, but it could be warmer," she replied. "I told you my last name. How about you tell me yours. And tell me about your wife."

"That will be hard," I said. I told her that "Joe" was not my real name and went on with a capsule version of my situation. I finished by looking at my wedding ring and saying, "I am ashamed to tell you I can't even remember my wife. Isn't that a crime?"

"That's not your fault, Joe," she said. She paused for a minute and continued, "I admit to being on the prowl, checking out men. I've been studying you and wishing you didn't have that ring. You are a nice man, Joe, and your wife will find you. If you were my husband I would hunt you to the end of the earth!" Kitty paused here for nearly a minute, and then continued, "My husband is lying dead on Guadalcanal. He was a marine, one of the first to die – God, I hate this war!"

Kitty was sobbing and I held her close until our break was over. To have this beautiful woman in my arms was – well, I can't think of proper words to describe it. She was so frank, so adorable, so tempting, and so off limits! She was trouble with a capital "T." As we walked back to our work area, Kato emerged from the medical library and seeing us walking side by side, gave me a knowing look. How quickly a feeling of guilt can destroy a beautiful illusion.

7/13/43 Kitty again sought me out at break time. It was a unique experience to be pursued by a woman, especially a beautiful woman. It was a reversal of some natural order and I loved it. She wanted to be my lover and she said so. She did most of the talking and I absorbed every word. I learned about her husband, her parents, her sisters, and I told her about Kan and "G" and my tribal friends. We met again on the afternoon break. Her magic was working; I was falling in love!

7/18/43 It was Sunday again. It was warm on deck and both chaplains were conducting nondenominational services. We had passed the equator and the sea was calm. Dolphins followed alongside and the ever-present "gooney birds" circled overhead. It was a blissful scene.

I was changing the dressing on a soldier's leg when I felt a soft hand on my shoulder. It was Kitty. She was her usual brightly smiling pretty self. "Hi," she said, and I dropped my spool of gauze on the deck. Kitty retrieved it for me and apologized for surprising me. As I removed the soiled portion from the roll I tried to get a grip on myself. Quite frankly I had become infatuated with the woman and she was standing there, only inches away. I was spellbound and tongue-tied. Fortunately, the soldier I was treating came to my rescue with a long line of banter directed at Kitty, to which she happily responded. This gave me time to complete work and calm my nerves.

Ever since the previous Monday I had struggled with adulterous thoughts and sleepless nights. Kato sensed my turmoil and gently reminded me that I would soon find my wife. He did not need to tell me what a happy reunion that would be if I were free of guilt. I knew that full well! But Kitty was here now, and apparently so willing, so available! I felt like a kite in the wind, at the whim of forces beyond my control. I was a wreck!

Completing my work, I stood erect and looked Kitty in the eye. "We need to talk," I said and she nodded in agreement. We found a place that was far enough away from others so that we could talk freely. I could feel the heat of her body, even though we were not touching. The urge to take her in my arms was overwhelming, yet another force was at work as well. My brain was a war zone! "I've had a hell of a week, Kitty," I whispered.

"Me too," she replied, "I want you so bad, Joe, and I can see what I am doing to you. I hate myself for that. I am tempting you to break your vows, and that is a sin, a terrible sin. You have a wife waiting to see you, and I am acting like a home wrecker. Can you forgive me, Joe?"

"Of course. We have done nothing wrong, not yet anyway. And it's true, if we did, we would both suffer in the end. Strange, the power this little gold band has." I said as I held up my left hand. "Half of me would give my life to make love to you, but the ring says, 'FORGET IT, SOLDIER!' No one has ever tempted me the way you do, Kitty. If we can behave ourselves, we can move on, without guilt, to someone we can love. Oh, but you will always be one hell of a memory, Kitty!"

We must have stood there in silence for ten minutes, leaning on the railing, watching the dolphins, but not seeing them. Finally Kitty spoke, "God! You sound like a minister, Joe. You are right, of course. I will postpone my husband hunting until after I get back to Toledo, then WATCH OUT! Thanks for letting me down easy, Joe. You're a good man. Please forgive me."

"Kitty, for the first time in a week, I feel like a good man too," I answered. "Now I have other wounds to patch up." I reached out my hand and grasped hers in a handshake. It was a brother-sister handshake, and we looked each other straight in the eye as we did it. It felt good! "See you around," I said.

"Right," she replied, and gave me a wonderful smile, sprinkled with teardrops. It was over.

7/19/43 A few of our wounded lived in Hawaii, so our ship docked there during the night. In the morning we expected to see something akin to the pictures on travel posters. What we saw instead was a scene of unbelievable destruction; a harbor littered with wrecked ships, far worse than the harbor at Port Moresby. No one was given leave and we were under way again that evening. Next stop: San Francisco!

7/21/43 We passed under the Golden Gate Bridge and slowly crept into dock. We were home, or so they say. There was music and laughter everywhere. Some nurses were allowed to leave with patients, but most of us were held to the end. Kato and I were heading for the gangplank when Kitty appeared beside us, duffle bag slung over her shoulder and her cap askew. She kissed us both and disappeared in the crowd. I shall always remember Kitty as I saw her that day.

CHAPTER THIRTEEN
RECOLLECTIONS BY ANDY

9/10/43 I was just closing up my repair shop for the day when Birdie walked in and plunked himself down in a chair. His flight jacket was wet and he looked beat. "I just landed and I got plenty to tell you. Let's find a quiet bar with good food. I'm starved!" he said.

"And I have a million questions – like, did you find Rick and where is Mattie?" I said.

"Mattie's with her mum and dad. Hey, first things first. You'll get the whole story after I've settled my stomach. The air was bumpy as hell up there and to make matters worse, the heater quit on me! I'm freezing!" After a few seconds he nervously continued, "I haven't checked in yet. We need to talk before I do, so let's get out of here."

It was a miserable rainy evening, the tail end of winter. I knew just the bar that would have a roaring blaze in the fireplace and, I hoped, not many customers. Something was really bothering Birdie and I feared the news would be bad. I asked no more questions and soon we parked in the nearly empty parking lot and made a dash for the door. The place suited Birdie just fine and soon he was ready to talk.

What I heard was better than I expected. Rick was surely in the US by this time and even had a doctor as a traveling companion. Mattie had Australian Army authorization to travel to the States from Sydney and was with her parents for the time being. Things were falling into place; it was good news. Then he told me what was worrying him. "Just before I took off for New Guinea with Mattie, a courier brought me a sealed letter from Nash. In it he ordered me to report to him the moment I got back and report everything that took place. I did not tell Mattie this. I told Mattie that I would simply tell Nash that Rick was not in Port Moresby after all, and that she went home to live with her parents. But I just know that Nash will find out that Rick went to the States and that she is planning to go too. So I will either get busted for lying to Nash or I will kill Mattie's chances of catching up to Rick. He hates Mattie's guts and would override Colonel Farmer's authorization in a minute, just for spite. I am sure he would. So I'm twixt a rock and a hard place. Got any ideas, Andy? What would you do?"

"Birdie," I replied, "you have a wife and kids. You can't afford to get busted. Tell Nash the truth and if he does what you say, perhaps we can buy her a ticket on the black market. It won't be cheap, that's for sure." That seemed to ease Birdie's mind, so we were able to enjoy the steaks we had ordered. We had made a decision; a good one, we hoped. With the rain beating on the windows and the logs crackling in the fire, the remainder of our evening was delightful.

9/11/43 Birdie caught up with me in the mess hall. His meeting with Nash had gone as expected. General Nash had pretended to be delighted that Mattie was headed to the US to find her husband and Birdie got a pat on the back for his role. What Nash would do now remained to be seen.

I got on the phone with Barb and Pat and they invited Birdie and me for supper. Pat, calling himself the mess sergeant, had taken over as the cook. A carpenter had lowered the kitchen counters and modified the sink and stove so that Pat could work from his wheelchair. As Barb explained things, "I bring home the bacon and Pat fries it. I hate to cook and Pat loves it!" Well, if the baked bluefish dinner he served us was an example of his skill, he certainly earned his stripes!

The main topic of conversation, of course, was Mattie and Rick. Barb did not think that Nash would be mean enough to cancel Mattie's trip, but Birdie did not agree. After dinner we made a phone call to Mattie in Sydney and advised her to ship out as soon as possible. She gave us the address and phone number of Rick's parents in the States and I told her I would try to patch through a phone call to them. I said that if I was successful, it might be tomorrow, sometime shortly after midnight. I would call her back, our last connection, and she must be ready to talk. (Back then, calling half a world away was uncertain at best.)

9/12/43 This was a Sunday and in my radio shop I managed to hook Mattie up with the in-laws she had never met. It was early morning here so it was evening in Princeton, New Jersey, USA. Mattie called me back after the call to thank me and tell me what was said. The Billings were, of course, overjoyed to hear that their son was alive and somewhere in the States, and that they would finally get to meet Mattie. They felt that their prayers were being answered and they were confident that Rick would be found and made whole again.

It was all so inspiring that I closed the shop and hurried to the base chapel to catch the church service.

CHAPTER FOURTEEN
MATTIE'S DIARY

9/12/43 This morning I talked on the phone to Mum and Dad Billings in the United States of America! Andy managed to patch it through some place in South America I think. Whatever he did, it worked and they came through loud and clear. They even had to tell me to stop shouting and speak normally. They sound like such nice people and I can't wait to meet them in person.

Apparently Colonel Farmer had sent word to the US Army that Rick is alive and somewhere in the States. The US Army had advised the Billingses, or is it the Billings? The Billings's? I'd better get it right, it's my name too! Anyway they were glad to hear it from me too. They are checking the Army hospitals and doing a lot of praying they said.

Andy seemed afraid that Nash might cancel my travel authorization. The general may be a sick old womanizer, but I don't think he is that rotten. I will, however, leave tomorrow if I can find a ship, even though Mum (my mum) has been pleading with me to wait another week or so. Now I need to finish packing my duffle and Dad's old suitcase. I also need to find something "Australian" as a gift for the Billings, (?) something small, but nice.

9/13/43 I made a couple phone calls this morning and a shipping clerk told me of a ship that would leave tomorrow morning at 0900. He thought there might be a few berths left, but "get your butt here fast!" As we waited outside for the taxi (Mum and Dad had given up their car), my dear dad removed his beloved gold pocket watch, his engraved retirement gift after a lifetime on the railroad, and placed it in my hand. "I want this back," he said, smiling through tears, "And I want you to bring it yourself!" Mum – well, she was crying too hard to say much.

"Thanks Dad. I will treasure this and I will come home again," I promised, just as the taxi pulled into our driveway. I am glad it was over fast, because I couldn't have stood much more!

The ship had seen better days, perhaps as a cruise ship. They had a couple berths left in the woman's section so I had my papers stamped and was told to join a queue that was going on board. I was committed. No chance to go shopping for that gift. I was on my way!

Most of the people in line were old men and boys. When I stepped on deck and my papers were checked again, I was directed to follow another woman to cabin 46B. She was to be my roommate it turned out. From behind I could see that she was tall and slim with short blond hair. She carried a huge suitcase in one hand and a tennis racket in the other. When I followed her into the cabin, she turned and smiled. "Guess we're room-mates. I'm Sonya," she said. Her accent was Scandinavian I thought.

As we introduced ourselves and settled our gear, the prospect of having Sonya as a traveling companion was very pleasant indeed. She was a tennis player who got stranded in Australia when war broke out. She, like me, had a husband she was trying to reach. We shared our stories and compared notes. I had slept little the night before, so I lay down on my bed to take a nap before lunch. I was nearly asleep when the PA system boomed, "Will passenger Matilda Jones Billings report to the MP office, number 10A, immediately." It repeated three times and I remained transfixed in my place. My racing mind could only come to one conclusion: Nash had canceled my authorization! Sonya gave me a questioning look and I simply shook my head. "I have to hide," I whispered, and was about to rush from the cabin when Sonya put her strong arms about me.

"You're small. I think you will fit in my suitcase," she said. Immediately she emptied its contents and, without hesitation, I folded myself like a pretzel in the case and she snapped the lid. Having proven that I actually fit, she released the lid so I could breath. She quickly stowed the clothing from the case into the cabinet drawers that the ship provided. She was almost done when there was a loud knock on the door. Sonya closed the lid and shouted, "Just a minute till I get some clothes on," and after a suitable delay, opened the door. It was an MP and he wanted me. Sonya told him that she had met me, but that I had gone off to look over the ship. The MP said I was AWOL from the Coast Guard (not true of course. I was legally retired) and that I had to be caught before we sailed. Sonya expressed concern and vowed to help in my capture.

After he left and I was freed from my cramped quarters, Sonya laughed and said, "Now tell me what kind of devilment you've been up to." So I told her the whole story, every bit, and she just sat there shaking her head and saying, "Men, men, men!"

When lunch was announced for our section, Sonya took a little bag with her and brought food back for me to eat. I kept the suitcase ready in case we got another visit from the MPs, but they had more important crimes to solve and in the morning our ship began to move. I was out of General Nash's reach at last! Now I could show my face.

The threat from Japanese attack was far from over, of course. Each morning before sunrise we all gathered on deck beside our assigned lifeboat or raft and stood there until the sun was up, since this was the worst time for torpedo attacks. No light was allowed on deck at night and the ship changed direction often to confuse the enemy. We had a couple of depth charges at the ready, sitting on the fantail, in case we picked up a nasty follower.

With all the zigzagging we did, our trip lasted twenty-two days on the ocean. It was time enough to make some great friendships and it was also time enough for the MPs to find me if they wanted to; they did not. We docked in San Francisco during the wee hours of the morning, so I missed seeing the famous Golden Gate Bridge from underneath.

10/7/43 The bay was wrapped in a dense fog (Sonya called it "smog") as we stood side by side on the deck, waiting our turn to disembark. It was the parting of the ways for Sonya and me. She hoped to restart her tennis career and I promised to read the sports pages. She planned to fly to Texas, while I would take a train to New York City, where the Billings said they would meet me with their car.

Before we disembarked, several banks set up offices on deck to exchange our money (at a premium) and, they hoped, set up bank accounts. Sonya knew the ropes better than I, and like a mother hen, stayed by my side until I was safely on a train bound for the East Coast. I kissed her before stepping on board and she said, "Watch out for the men!"

CHAPTER FIFTEEN
JOE'S RECORD

7/21/43 When our turn finally came to leave the ship, the sun had set and Kato and I were starved. There was a queue for a meal at the nearby base, but we craved a fine dinner in a restaurant, so we left the line and headed out on our own. It was an unwise decision. We chose a Chinese restaurant and as we were guided to a table, a murmur of angry voices followed us. Almost immediately a tall man wearing the restaurant logo stepped up to our table and said we must leave. "No Japanese served here!" he spit out. I was about to retort, but Kato restrained me and we left. We then tried a steak house and got a similar rebuff. We were in dangerous territory! We had walked nearly a mile from the base mess, but turned around and got back just as they were closing the serving line. We had learned a lesson, and it was frightening.

7/22/43 We stayed on the base after that. We still had the wounded to care for until, one after another; they could be shipped to hospitals near their homes. On the base, Kato's rank of major had more relevance than the appearance of his face. On the street, it was the reverse. We soon learned of the Japanese internment camps that had been set up on the assumption that all Japanese are potential enemies! Why the Japanese and not the Germens or Italians? Kato Matsuri received his commission as a US Army major by way of a field commission from a US Army officer he had never met, at the request of an Australian Army colonel. It was legal, but rather complicated, and Kato had reason to worry. He was a good doctor and his reputation was sound, but yes, he had reason to worry.

My concerns were somewhat different. I wanted, needed, to stay with Kato both for his protection and my own. I had kept quiet about my amnesia. As long as I keep busy and did not attract attention, I seemed able to remain unnoticed. Once identified as a patient, I would certainly be whisked away to a treatment center, God knows where. Kato had a better idea: He wanted me to see a doctor in Boston, a Dr. Manville, who specialized in memory loss. He was a man whom Kato once met at Harvard and whose work he admired.

8/12/43 This base was sort of a way station for returning service men and women. The numbers varried, depending on the ships that arrived. The permanent cadre was rather small and relied heavily on help from the visitors. Most service personnel have, or are given, a destination to go to; Kato and I were an exception. The orders we received from Colonel Farmer got us to the States, but that's it. Sooner or later, the base CO, Colonel Moody, was bound to take notice of us. Finally he did just that and we were called to his office.

The colonel was an easygoing sort. He had time, he said, and wanted to hear the whole story, so we told him everything. He seemed genuinely interested and seemed envious of the adventures we had experienced. He said that he had been stuck in "this pest hole" for the entire war and craved a little action. He said he would like to have us stay on, but assumed we had some plans of our own. When he asked us what we would REALLY like to do next, Kato mentioned Dr. Manville in Boston, and Moody said he would try to arrange for us to meet.

We must have talked for over an hour and evening was approaching. Finally, he suggested we all go out to eat, his treat. Concerned about what might happen, we told him about our recent experience with bigots. "Then I know the perfect place," he said. Then looking Kato in the eye, he said, "I hope you like Japanese food. I know a quiet little place up in the hills that few people know about. I was there last week. Let's go."

The colonel drove his jeep, Kato up front, me in back. California gets cold at night, especially in the hills, and the chill easily penetrated my summer uniform, but the sight we saw as we rounded the final turn in the road was far more chilling! The restaurant had been burned to the ground, the ashes still smoldering in the night air! And as we approached, two pickup trucks, one bearing a large American flag, roared off into the darkness!

8/13/43 After the experience of the previous night, Kato and I planned to eat on base. Anyway, another ship was about to debark, and we were very busy preparing for wounded marines. We did what we could to make their homecoming pleasant. Most of the bedridden men needed assistance making a phone call home. I tried not to listen, but I heard anyway, and I wondered what I might say if I were calling a home I've forgotten, to a wife I cannot remember. It was a dreadful thought! I tried to shake it, but it persisted.

8/17/43 Kato and I were paged to come to the colonel's office, "at your convenience." (How many CO's would be so undemanding?) As we entered he said, "Hey, I have some good news for you. This Dr. Manville is waiting to see you, Joe, and he remembers you, Kato, as the bright college kid who asked so many questions one night that he nearly missed his train! I took the liberty of getting you a ride in a B-17 that is leaving LA at 0900 tomorrow and will drop you in Boston. Here is the doctor's address, phone number and your travel papers. My driver will take you to the airport at 0600. Think you can make it?"

When we assured him that we were delighted, he suggested a drink in the Officers' Club. After we were settled, he said he had some advice. "I like the way you two watch out for each other," he said. "You may both be dying to get out of the army, I know that I am, but don't jump at the chance. Kato, in the service you are a damn good doctor, but as a civilian, you will be busted back to a student again and could even wind up in one of those interment camps! Think about it! And you, Joe, you get your head reattached and find your wife. That's my fatherly advice for today. Drink up!"

It was sound advice, but no different than what we had decided ourselves. We talked about our plans for after the war – how we might restart our lives. Moody was unmarried, about the same age as Kato, and eager to see the world. He had studied civil engineering – maybe he could help rebuild the cities broken by war. Kato was interested in medical research and I felt sure would be famous some day. I hardly needed to say what I wanted. I wanted to be whole again. But after that I wanted to return to Papua and find my dear young friend, Kan, and shake the big hand of "G" to whom I owed my very life.

It was a fine evening in all respects. Moody treated us to a huge steak dinner in the club and we finally parted with the obligatory promises to look each other up after the war.

8/18/43 The B-17 was a drafty beast so Kato and I were provided warm flight jackets for the trip. My old one had long since ended in the trash. Our pilot, a guy named Brian, flew low enough to the ground to avoid using oxygen masks. Knowing about my memory loss, Brian pointed out the items of interest below. He must have flown the route often because his spiel was endless – and grew quite tiresome. I sat in the copilot's seat and felt a definite urge to take the controls, which led me to the conclusion that I must have been a pilot myself, not just a passenger. Another piece of the puzzle had fallen into place!

We landed and spent the night at a military airport near Kansas City. I was quite tired and turned in early. I slept well despite the frequent roar of aircraft; at least Brian was not talking!

8/20/43 Brian was a good pilot and as we got closer to the East Coast, he spent most of his time on the radio, talking to first one tower and then the next, and staying clear of congested air space. We were traveling toward the sun, so evening came on quickly, and it was quite dark when we landed in the Boston area.

Brian had to turn the bomber over to the Army Air Force (it was headed to England) and then take a train back to California. He said he knew a great hotel and restaurant, so after he was free, we let him lead the way. Well, Brian's "great hotel" was more of a dive, or worse. I looked at Kato and he shook his head; we wanted something better. We wished Brian a good trip back and grabbed a taxi into the city.

8/21/43 Saturday, and we had a weekend to kill. We left the air-conditioned hotel and walked into an adjoining park. It was lovely with large trees and flowers everywhere. The weather was very hot and humid with on-again-off-again showers; quite a change from California. This was Kato's city so we set out to visit some of his favorite haunts.

There was no question about what the first stop would be: Kato's sweetheart, Virginia Mansuka. Kato and Ginny met at a discussion group at Harvard. Both of Japanese heritage, they just "fell together" as Kato expressed it. Born in the States, Ginny's parents picked a name with an American sound. A political science major, Ginny would have probably been graduated by this time.

It was much too far to walk and Kato knew just which bus to take. After our experience in California we were braced for hostility, but nothing happened; Easterners were more accepting. The bus was a local and made many stops, but finally we came to Ginny's street. The homes here were modest, but most were neatly cared for with little fenced in front yards. The Mansuka home was an exception; it was deserted with plywood panels covering the windows. The grass was uncut and a realtor's sign had been attached to one of the panels. Kato stared in disbelief. "They've moved!" he said to himself.

"Well, people do move," I responded. "We should have checked the phone book before we came. Let's find a pay phone and call that realtor."

Well, in the end we returned to the hotel, with the blessed air conditioning, and made a call from there. What Kato discovered was distressing indeed! The entire Mansuka family had been relocated to an internment camp in Arkansas. There was a phone number he might call to make contact, but the realtor, hearing Kato's name, strongly advised against calling. "You might wind up there yourself," he said. "Nobody has a private phone there. They would be called to the camp director's office to take your call. Just imagine how risky that is. Mail gets read too. Don't say I didn't warn you!" It was chilling news for poor Kato and I feared he might disregard the man's advice and call anyway.

We were about to go outside again, but found that a thunderstorm was beginning. The weather seemed to reflect our mood exactly. Changing our mind, we settled in the lounge instead. In the past, Kato had spoken little to me about his personal life, his parents, or Ginny and her parents, but now he opened up. He had pent-up feelings bursting to get out and I felt honored to be trusted with them. He told me about his father and the sharp division between them. His father was loyal to the Emperor, and expressed a deep hatred of the United States, whereas his mother secretly supported Kato and the choices he had made. It was his mother who spent her own personal inheritance to send Kato to the US and Harvard University; his father would have no part in it! In fact, Kato had good reason to believe that during his untimely visit home, his father had instigated his induction into the Japanese Army!

Ginny, in fact her entire family, he said, were so very like his own mother in disposition and character, that he felt entirely at peace in their presence. Ginny and he would surely be married and be extremely happy if only they could find each other again.

8/22/43 Sunday. The air today was fresh and pleasant after the rain. We wandered about the Harvard campus and the parks where Kato had gone as a student to find peace and tranquility. For lunch we entered a tiny sandwich shop, a student hangout, where the owner remembered Kato and greeted him warmly. Then sitting on a bench by the Charles River, Kato described the work of Dr. Manville, and why it so impressed him. On Monday we would meet the man in person.

8/23/43 Colonel Moody had calculated our arrival in Boston correctly and had even made our doctor's appointment. We were there at 0900 hours and the doctor was waiting for us. He had no receptionist or secretary. The furnishings were old-fashioned and seemed quite appropriate for the doctor, who appeared to be in his seventies. After we were seated he offered us coffee that he apparently had brewed himself.

He made a rather cursory inspection of my wound, made a few notes and settled down to talk. He asked me questions on every possible subject, some quite embarrassing, like my close encounter with Kitty. He tested my knowledge in various fields, such as world geography, government, mineral deposits, you name it. His face expressed no emotion from my responses, but he watched me closely as I spoke. He seemed to be looking inside my brain, seeing how it worked. He included Kato in a discussion of Japan, Germany, and Italy. He probed the treatment of Jews, Negroes, and Mexicans. He was searching for my prejudices and sore points; he asked about my opinions.

By noon I think he had reached some of the same conclusions as Mad Moe, but he kept them to himself. He did reassure me that Colonel Moody had arranged for the army to pay the cost of his service. We were scheduled to meet every weekday morning for one month. He said he had made progress already, although I could not imagine how. Was it something I said?

Kato suggested that we get lunch at the Harvard cafeteria. It was summer session so the student numbers were low. Kato had been away too long to recognize any of the students, but got a warm reception from several of the professors. One man, a Dr. Burnett, gave Kato some information that altered the course of his life! The US Army, he said, had been forming the 442nd Infantry in Tennessee composed of Nisei (Japanese born in the United States). They were slated to go to fight in Europe – a chance to prove their proclaimed loyalty to the United States! Their motto, he said, was "GO FOR BROKE." True, strictly speaking, Kato was not Nisei, but he was already a US Army doctor. He would surely qualify!

Kato by nature was quiet and not demonstrative. Now, however, he leapt to his feet and did a little dance, something he learned from the Peace Trekkers perhaps. This was just what he wanted! Doctor Burnett advised him not to delay. If he wanted to sign up, he should do it today.

After thanking the professor profusely, we found a shaded bench on the campus and sat down to think this through. Kato had not yet looked up Dr. Marty Goldenberg, the old friend of Colonel Farmer's, and that weighed on him a little. I argued that time was of the essence and he should go this very day! In my mind it was a fait accompli and we no longer truly needed each other. For us it was a natural parting of the ways. Then I had a great idea. "You might even find Ginny there!" I suggested.

"I already thought of that, that is ALL I've been thinking about!" he said. "Why did you think I was dancing?"

Well, I won't drag this out. Kato and I found a recruiting office that afternoon where he filed a request for reassignment to the 442nd Infantry. It was granted, just like that! A jeep took us to the hotel so he could get his duffle, and then to a train bound for Tennessee. I reported to the hotel bar for a stiff drink! I would miss Kato – badly.

8/24/43-9/24/43 Doctor Manville and I have met each weekday morning for this entire month with little to show for it. He agrees that I am probably a pilot, probably an officer. He found no record of an Australian company named "Outback Adventures" having ever existed, though it was painted on my parachute. Manville had hoped to develop "links in the brain," but I was apparently a difficult case. His final recommendation for me was to be seen by some researchers at Dartmouth College who were studying trauma cases for the military. He gave me a letter of introduction and a review of the work he had done. Quite frankly, I was losing hope. The good doctor wrote down all the directions for me. He was a nice old man and he certainly did his best.

I had been living at a local Navy base to save money. They used me in the mess hall during the afternoons and the food was far better than the Army chow. This would be my last weekend in Boston. It would be nice to do something different for a change.

9/27/43 Monday. I took a Greyhound bus north to Dartmouth College in Hanover, New Hampshire. Upon my arrival, I found the research lab that Manville had directed me to and checked in. It was on the Dartmouth campus, associated with the Dartmouth Medical School, but run by the army.

The director said he had great respect for Dr. Manville and referred to him as a pioneer in the field, but said new tools had resulted in new breakthroughs. He said the therapy involved a degree of physical stress, but it should be easily tolerated. He gave me a tour of the lab and let me use the rest room. There on the wall over the sink was a cartoon showing a man in a white coat swinging a huge mallet at a man's head. The caption read, "WE CRACK NUTS." It was tasteless and crude. It was supposed to be funny, but it made me uneasy. I did, of course, agree to the treatments they recommended and went to find a room at a hotel. I had a few days to kill before the work began.

9/28/43 I stopped in at the Office of Student Housing to compare dorm prices with those of the hotel. (Since it remained uncertain whether I was a soldier or a civilian, the Army paid me subsistence, but required that I buy my own room and meals.) At the housing office, I was offered a dorm room to share with an engineering student at a much lower price, so I said "Yes" without hesitation.

It was a good decision. My roommate's name was Mark Dugan, class of '45. He was tall, thin, and serious minded. He appeared delighted to share space with me, an older man, assuming, he said with a smile, I would not have wild parties and play loud music. I assured him that he had nothing to fear.

Mark expressed his regret that I had missed the previous Saturday's football season opener with Holy Cross, which "we" had won, 3-0. The next game would be with the Coast Guard and we could go together. I hated to disappoint him, but I said, "Thanks, but no thanks." I wanted to settle in, find a good used typewriter, and organize my thoughts. I planned to begin writing my memoirs, using the scattered notes I had made in Kato's diary book and various scraps of paper I used after the book was filled up. I relished the prospect of this free time before starting therapy on the following Monday.

Mark was understanding and even said he knew a friend who had received a new typewriter for his birthday, and might still have his old one for sale. Sooner or later, Mark insisted, I would have to go to one of the games, and to that, I agreed.

9/29/43 Mark went with me to the college cafeteria for breakfast, to show me the ropes. The food was excellent, and inexpensive, so I planned to eat all my meals there during my stay. Mark had to rush to a class, so I walked back to the dorm alone and found the door standing wide open, and another young man sitting at my desk! At first I thought I might be in the wrong room, but no, it was Mark's friend with the typewriter. It was an Underwood portable and he wanted ten bucks, but the price was negotiable, he said. He even included an extra ribbon. I felt it should have cost a lot more, but I accepted his price and we shook hands on it. I paid him and he rushed off to a class, leaving me to commence the journal you see here. It would be a challenge, but it might even help solve my terrible memory loss.

10/10/43 This was a Sunday, my day of rest and I needed it. I had completed my first week of therapy and, as the director warned me, the therapy was stressful, both physically and mentally. It was supposed to awaken pre-trauma memory. All it had awakened was a feeling of despair. Initially I was full of hope, but I had to admit, I had a terrible urge to run away and become a hermit somewhere; just disappear completely! I believed I was a member of the military (based on Dr. Manville's work) and that I was one of hundreds, maybe thousands, of missing soldiers, most of them dead. Thinking rationally, could I expect my wife to still be waiting for my return? Surely she had given up and moved on.

In the morning I would begin another week of therapy. The sessions ran all morning, giving me the afternoon to rest up and, if I was not too tired, work on my journal. I wouldn't have minded if I felt it was going somewhere. After the next week, if I still felt the same way, I considered following my instinct to drop out.

Mark, who was a Quaker, was the son of a dairy farmer in Ohio. At Mark's suggestion, his father had offered me a job on the farm and, in addition, the Friends School in their community might, I say might, take me on as a teacher despite my obvious shortcomings. It was tempting.

CHAPTER SIXTEEN
MATTIE'S DIARY

10/7/43 This has been one incredible day. This morning Sonya and I were still on the ship and now I am whizzing through the night on a train heading east. Sonya got me on a sleeper so I wouldn't have to sleep sitting up. I was too excited to sleep just then, but I know I should go to bed soon. I am not sure what time it is; Dad's watch only tells me the time back home. When I called the Billings they predicted I would get to New York on the 9th or 10th, depending on how many delays we get. I'm to call when I get to Chicago.

10/8/43 This was our second wedding anniversary and I was sitting there all teary while, outside the window, the scenery was absolutely gorgeous. I should not have been crying, but I couldn't help it. Somewhere out there, outside my window, Rick was waiting to be found, and I would find him, I was sure! Even if I had to walk through all the hospitals in the United States, I would find him! It might take years, but I would never stop until his arms were around me again. God what arms!

It was about then that a woman, about Mum's age, sat down beside me and put an arm around me. Through my tears I could see that she was a nun, so I explained that I wasn't a Catholic, and she just said it didn't matter one bit. So I just let go and soon I was cried out and able to talk. She didn't pry, but I told her everything. It was like having Mum there, only better, because Mum would have been sobbing too! After I got control of myself, I thanked her profusely and expected her to leave, but she stayed beside me for most of the day. We found a lot to talk about.

She was so nice and upbeat. Soon we were both enjoying the scenery and chatting about that instead of my troubles. We had been going through the Rocky Mountains and boy they were something! She said that Chinese laborers, many years ago, built much of the track by hand. I was impressed!

10/9/43 I hoped to visit with my new friend again, but she was not to be seen. Perhaps she was comforting some one else in need. She was such a lovely woman.

Our train was moved to a siding to let a long freight train go by. It was loaded with army trucks and guns and required two engines to pull it. So much machinery devoted to war! When will it stop?

10/10/43 We arrived in Chicago and I had to change trains to a coach called a "Flier." I called Mum and Dad Billings and gave them the listed arrival time in New York City. It will be tonight, after midnight, but they said they did not mind. They were so nice!

10/11/43 The Billings saw me the moment I stepped off the train. They were surprised to see I had only Dad's suitcase and my small duffle bag. Dad Billings said his wife would have had at least five, but I was sure he was kidding. They have a large Buick and insisted that I sit on the front seat, with Mum in the back, so I could "see better." Actually all I wanted to see were the Billings, so I twisted around so we could talk.

Mum, it turned out, was my match when it came to gabbing. Dad did not say much until I mentioned my encounter with Sonya. Sonya was really famous it turned out, was "top seed," or something like that. Dad, I was learning, is a sports history buff; knows all the players and the scores by heart.

10/12/43 The Billings' home is lovely and they have a beautiful garden with tall trees that are now turning red. It is on a quiet street with similar homes. I got up early and found a garden seat in the morning sun, a perfect spot to do my diary and contemplate the man who grew up here, who sat in this very seat! No wonder Rick grew up to be such a wonderful guy.

I was awakened from my reverie by a call from the house; breakfast was ready. Last night we avoided the subject of Rick, for fear that it might be too emotional. Now it was time. I heard about the steps they were taking to find him and I told them about what I had found out from my friends, and from Colonel Farmer. The Billings had already followed the colonel's advice, to call Harvard University. This, however, was a dead end; the university has no Major Kato Matsuri on their staff or their student roster. Phoning Army hospitals also was clearly pointless, but they did it anyway, they said.

Dad proudly showed me the trophies Rick won on the rowing team during his Princeton days. Oh! And I saw all of Rick's baby photos from Mum's endless supply. He was mighty cute, back when he was "Little Ricky."

Next up was a tour of the town and the university buildings and lunch at Dad's club. Dad, also a Princeton grad, was in his element here. Fall classes were in session so we just peeked into rooms. I found the beautiful grounds much more interesting and felt like exploring a bit on my own. In addition, I had seen a drugstore and needed to purchase a few personal items. I was wondering how to politely leave them when Mum read my thoughts. Speaking for Dad's benefit, she said, "I think Mattie might like a little time on her own. Am I right, Mattie? Do you remember the way back to the house? Supper will be at six; we're having pork chops." Mum gave me a knowing look and a kiss. I thanked her and I wandered in the direction of the lake that I had glimpsed between the trees earlier. It was 2 PM by my dad's gold watch (properly reset). I just wanted to sit quietly by the water for a while because my mind was racing. This lake had been Rick's playground. I dipped my finger in the water – it was icy. It was symbolic I guess, touching something of Rick's.

I stood up and started back. I should have brought a sweater. The sun was now behind a cloud and a chill breeze had sprung up. By the time I reached the drugstore I felt chilled through and was delighted to see Princeton sweatshirts for sale. I immediately bought one and put it on. It was bright orange with black letters and it felt warm and cozy. I pondered the gift that I had wanted to give the Billings, but nothing in the store was suitable. Perhaps, if I hurried back to Mum I could at least help with supper.

Mum saw me as I walked up the path and was waiting at the door. She seemed to love my shirt and said Dad had one just like mine, except a larger size. Now I would have to learn the Princeton songs and cheers she said. When I offered to help with supper she said she put it on the stove already; only thing left to do was eat it, she said. Then, lowering her voice, she said, "Come into my den where we can talk privately. I want to know more about your family, more than what they look like. After the war we plan to go to Australia so we can meet them, and all your friends. We have traveled about the world some, but never to Australia or New Zealand."

It was just what I needed, a warm room and a person who could talk with no holds barred. We poured out our souls to each other right up to suppertime. Only Barb, back home, was so free and open as Mum Billings, and it made me truly part of their family. From Mum I learned about Dad's exasperating habit of spending so much of their time together with his head in the newspaper, totally absorbed with the stock market and the sports pages. I told her about my dad's endless stories about his life as a railroad man, and she said she envied my mum! I showed her my gold pocket watch and told her what Dad (my dad) had said, and she hugged me, and we had a good cry together. I told her about Mum's sober view of life and how much I loved her anyway. Mum Billing's comment: she needs a good hugging!

Dad made a fire in the big fieldstone fireplace that evening. He said the radio predicted frost. Then Mum turned off all the lights so we could better enjoy the beauty of the fire. Dad grumbled a little about not being able to read the paper and Mum said, "That's all you ever do, dear!" whereupon Dad smiled and stretched out on the floor beside us. It was a lovely evening!

10/13/43 Mum and Dad had gotten a list of all the military hospitals and clinics in the United States, together with the address and phone number. The list was huge. For a time they had telephoned, but now they had a better plan: first, they typed up a form letter, that was direct and to the point, and had it mimeographed. Second, they had prints made of their best photograph of Rick in his Army uniform, hundreds of them. When I came down for breakfast today, I found Mum and Dad engaged in "step three," so I joined the assembly line, sealing and gluing stamps on envelopes with a damp sponge.

After breakfast we went back to it again, helped along by music on the record player. Every so often we would switch jobs to prevent boredom, but the realization that the VERY LETTER you were working on might be the one to find Rick – that was enough to keep us moving. We had a large cardboard box that we would fill to the top with completed letters each day and take to the post office. The postmaster had warned Mr. Billings that this was the most they could process per day, so that controlled the pace of our work.

10/30/43 This was football season, and Dad was always in the stands when Princeton played. The season had been cut back, because of the war, to only four Princeton games, so each game was even more important to him. Today, with Princeton not playing, he sat glued to the radio listening to Dartmouth play Yale. (Dartmouth won 20 to 6.) When I asked Mum about it, she just rolled her eyes! Dad was Dad.

Two Princeton games had already been played before my arrival, Penn State and Columbia I believe, and Dad felt badly that I missed them. I've never seen what Americans call "football," but the next game will be with Yale on November 13th, and I am expected to be there, no ifs or buts, fair weather or foul! In preparation, I have had a crash course in the rules and strategies of the game. Dad does not want a dummy sitting beside him! Mum just rolled her eyes.

11/12/43 My how time flies! Tomorrow will be my introduction to American football and I admit, I am a little nervous. Mum said, "Just do what Dad does, cheer when he cheers and act unhappy when he does. Be VERY careful not to cheer when Yale scores a point! And dress warm."

11/13/43 Well, I survived the game and I am in bed trying to warm up. It was quite a day. We had to drive a long distance in the car, and the car was warm, but the stadium was freezing! I was wearing all the clothes I owned plus some of Mum's. Mum had an old blanket for us to sit on, and several thermoses of hot chocolate and coffee, plus sandwiches for our lunch. That helped.

Yale beat Princeton 27 to 6 causing Dad to be unhappy. He got very excited throughout the game and yelled himself hoarse, but when I acted unhappy too, I did not need to pretend. Hey, anyway, it was a great game, I guess.

11/19/43 Princeton will play another game tomorrow, this time with Dartmouth. That will be the last one and (I hope Dad never reads this) I am glad! It will be held here and the weather is predicted to be mild. I have been thinking of sneaky ways I might use to not go, but Mum says it would break Dad's heart. I don't want that to happen, so I will be good and go to the game.

11/20/43 I enjoyed this game better than the last one. Dad looked unhappy because Dartmouth beat us, so I had to be careful not to look too happy. The weather was so warm that it felt more like late November in Australia, so for me, it was kind of like a short trip home. I will write Mum and Dad a nice long letter tonight. Now, Mum Billings is calling me to supper.

CHAPTER SEVENTEEN
JOE'S RECORD

11/14/43 Six weeks ago today, I began pondering the offer of farm work made by Mark's father, and giving up on the therapy sessions. The remote possibility of teaching at a Friends school also intrigued me, of course. Well, the pondering was over. I wrote Mark's father that I would take the job, and I formally resigned from the therapy program. I would go to the Dartmouth-Princeton game next Saturday, as I promised Mark I would, and then travel home with him to Ohio for Thanksgiving as his guest. I have finally made a firm decision and I feel good about it.

11/20/43 What an amazing day this has been! The chartered buses left the Dartmouth campus very early in the morning. It was the last game of the year, and spirits were high. I wore a Dartmouth sweatshirt, suggested by Mark to help me blend in, but I know I looked oddly out of place. I think I was twice their age, although I could not prove it. I was sure some thought I was an instructor.

Driving a busload of boisterous college boys certainly requires a calm disposition. Some of the antics of these students were hard for me to take. The loud shouting was enough to damage my eardrums. Was I ever like that as a boy? I tried to visualize how peaceful my new life would be, working with cows, as a farm hand. Mark did his best to encourage me, telling me stories about his childhood on the farm and how beautiful it was with a stream winding through the property.

We did finally arrive at the Princeton campus, and to avoid being crushed to death, Mark and I let the others scramble out first. As I walked by the driver I thanked him and said, "How do you keep so calm and cool?"

"I'm a Boy Scout Master! Do that a few years and you can handle anything! Keep your ticket. We leave at 8 PM sharp."

It was a beautiful warm day, a pleasant surprise this late in the fall, a bit of Indian Summer perhaps. As I emerged from the staircase into the stadium, I had a strange sense that I might have been there before. "Then again," a little voice told me, "If you have seen one stadium, you have seen them all. Stop making yourself even crazier than you already are!"

It was a great game and once I let myself get caught up in the spirit of it, I found myself yelling and cheering along with everyone else. We won 42 to 13 and as the game progressed, I learned one more thing about myself: I am an American, not an Australian. This is a game I know, a game I have played!

With the game over, Mark wanted to celebrate with several of his classmates. A big noisy party was planned for us under a tent on the campus. Mark urged me to join in, but I wanted to go for a walk, maybe find a quiet place to sit, so I excused myself and said I would meet them at the bus at 7:45.

The stadium was near the lake and I turned in that direction. The air was still warm – almost like summer. I walked down to the university boathouse and sat down on a bench facing the water. The sun was getting low in the sky, creating dramatic shadows on everything it touched. The surface of the lake was so still that the trees on the far shore, which were now bare of leaves, were reflected clearly in the water. It was the kind of scene that painters love, and it was a scene I had seen before! The whole place felt familiar to me. I tend to remember rustic places better than buildings and streets. I was onto something!

I was pondering these thoughts when a voice behind me said, "Hi! Mind if I join you on the bench? Why – it's Ricky Billings, back from the war! Ricky, how nice to see you, man! Are you home on leave? And what's with the Dartmouth sweatshirt?" I must have looked uncomprehending, to say the least. "Ricky, surely you remember me – it's Coach Thompson." I could hardly speak, but I slowly began to understand that he had NOT mistaken me for someone else. He KNEW me and had spoken my name, Ricky Billings! That was my name, Ricky Billings! The name I had been searching for, and it sounded right.

I had hurt the poor man's feelings, my old coach's feelings. I reached for his hand and held it as I stammered out the tale of my recent life, my memory loss. Tears trickled down the old man's cheeks as he told how he remembered all his boys. Our crew was the last he had coached before retirement. He often came here on nice days, he said, to warm himself and to reminisce. How wonderful that he had come today!

I asked him what else he could tell me about myself, to help me remember. "Come to my house," he said. "It's just up the road." As we stood and walked together, I could see how small and frail the old man was. His pace was slow, but he kept his body erect and, as he talked, his deep forceful voice began to penetrate my brain. I could hear him now counting out the cadence as we dipped the oars. It was coming back!

His home was small, but neatly cared for. In the living room one entire wall was given over to memorabilia about his "boys." In my section were my team records, several photos, and an article from the newspaper saying I had risen from lieutenant to captain in the US Army in the Southwest Pacific Theater of Operations – so, I am a captain!

Then he said, "Have you seen your mom and dad? No, I suppose not. They live right here in Princeton. I meet your dad on campus occasionally. Let's look up their address and surprise them!" With that he pulled out a phone book and looked it up. "Let's go! Maybe we will be right on time for supper," he said with a wide grin.

It was a long walk, but Coach Thompson kept up his steady pace. He seemed as excited about our meeting as I was. I am ashamed to say I was still trying to form the image of my parents in my sluggish brain when we entered the front walk.

At the front door I hesitated, trying to calm my pounding heart. "Well, ring the damn doorbell!" he said, a bit louder than necessary. I pressed the button and waited. After what seemed like an eternity, I rang it again. There were footsteps, a latch turned and the door swung open – it was Dad!

"It's Coach Thompson, Dear," he shouted. "Come in, Coach, so nice to see you." Dad never even looked in my direction!

"Thanks, I will," Thompson replied. "I brought a friend, someone I think you know." Now Dad looked my way and things clicked!

"Oh my God," he shouted. "Everyone come quick! It's Rick, he's here!"

Dad's bear hug came first, followed by Mom's tearful embrace. They both looked the way my sluggish mind had finally pictured them. My brain was healing!

Then I heard a rumble of feet on the stairs and a beautiful young woman leaped into my arms. Somewhere in my brain the final valve clicked shut and the circuits began to flow again. "I love you, Mattie," I whispered, "Thank you for waiting."

FINAL WORDS
BY ANDY

11/20/2010 Today is the 67th anniversary of that momentous day when Mattie and Rick were reunited! That was sixty-seven years ago and a lot has happened since. The following, in brief, is what occurred:

Rick returned to active service, made major, and was assigned to a desk job in the States. As soon as the war was over the entire Billings family sailed to Australia. Mattie's parents met Rick's parents and got along just fine. The elder Billings liked it so much, they settled in Melbourne.

Mattie and Rick still live in the old house. Mattie resumed her career in botanical research and Rick was invited back to teaching at Melbourne Academy. In the summers they traveled a lot – together! Believe me, Mattie didn't let Rick out of her sight!

One of their first trips was to Papua to visit "G" and Kan, and I traveled with them. What an emotional scene that was! Mattie and Rick presented Kan with a complete set of schoolbooks for use in the school that the young prince had begun for tribal children. Kan was overjoyed. "G" smiled appreciatively and raised his right forefinger.

Kato and Ginny survived the war and were married while in service. Kato fulfilled his goal of doing medical research and was highly regarded in his field.

Barb and Pat have two children, a girl and a boy, and I am "Uncle Andy." Pat still enjoys cooking and I get treated like a member of the family.

I never married. I re-upped in the Australian Army, and made master sergeant. Now, retired, I do a little writing.

THE END